"I'm not one of your patients, Edie."

Holden bit out the words. "Platitudes and encouraging pats on the back are not what *I* need from you."

She shook her head, trying to clear it as she drew in a shuddering breath, which brought her breasts flush up against him.

She saw the havoc her action wreaked on his composure. On his ability to remain detached and in control, which was so blasted important to him, and not just as a physician.

Fully knowing what she was doing, she took another lung-filling breath. His gaze burned into hers.

Edie didn't pull away. Couldn't turn away, and not because she had promised herself she wouldn't.

"What *do* you need from me, then, Holden?"

Dear Reader,

Silhouette Romance novels aren't just for other women—the wonder of a Silhouette Romance is that it can touch *your* heart. And this month's selections are guaranteed to leave you smiling!

In Suzanne McMinn's engaging BUNDLES OF JOY title, *The Billionaire and the Bassinet,* a blue blood finds his hardened heart irrevocably tamed. This month's FABULOUS FATHERS offering by Jodi O'Donnell features an emotional, heartwarming twist you won't soon forget; in *Dr. Dad to the Rescue,* a man discovers strength and the healing power of love from one *very* special lady. *Marrying O'Malley,* the renegade who'd been her childhood nemesis, seemed the perfect way for a bride-to-be to thwart an unwanted betrothal—until their unlikely alliance stirred an even more incredible passion; don't miss this latest winner by Elizabeth August!

The Cowboy Proposes...Marriage? Get the charming lowdown as WRANGLERS & LACE continues with this sizzling story by Cathy Forsythe. Cara Colter will make you laugh and cry with *A Bride Worth Waiting For,* the story of the boy next door who *didn't* get the girl, but who'll stop at nothing to have her now. For readers who love powerful, dramatic stories, you won't want to miss *Paternity Lessons,* Maris Soule's uplifting FAMILY MATTERS tale.

Enjoy this month's titles—and please drop me a line about *why* you keep coming back to Romance. I want to make sure we continue fulfilling *your* dreams!

Regards,

Mary-Theresa Hussey
Senior Editor Silhouette Romance

Please address questions and book requests to:
Silhouette Reader Service
U.S.: 3010 Walden Ave., P.O. Box 1325, Buffalo, NY 14269
Canadian: P.O. Box 609, Fort Erie, Ont. L2A 5X3

DR. DAD
TO THE RESCUE

Jodi O'Donnell

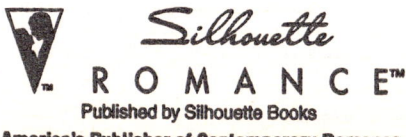

Published by Silhouette Books
America's Publisher of Contemporary Romance

If you purchased this book without a cover you should be aware that this book is stolen property. It was reported as "unsold and destroyed" to the publisher, and neither the author nor the publisher has received any payment for this "stripped book."

For my soul sisters, both human and canine.
You saved my life.

ACKNOWLEDGMENTS

My thanks to Tammy Hermanson for her help with the ins and outs of physical therapy, and to William R. Irey, M.D., for providing me with the technical descriptions on broken arms. Any errors are entirely my own.

 SILHOUETTE BOOKS

ISBN 0-373-19385-8

DR. DAD TO THE RESCUE

Copyright © 1999 by Jodi O'Donnell

All rights reserved. Except for use in any review, the reproduction or utilization of this work in whole or in part in any form by any electronic, mechanical or other means, now known or hereafter invented, including xerography, photocopying and recording, or in any information storage or retrieval system, is forbidden without the written permission of the editorial office, Silhouette Books, 300 East 42nd Street, New York, NY 10017 U.S.A.

All characters in this book have no existence outside the imagination of the author and have no relation whatsoever to anyone bearing the same name or names. They are not even distantly inspired by any individual known or unknown to the author, and all incidents are pure invention.

This edition published by arrangement with Harlequin Books S.A.

® and TM are trademarks of Harlequin Books S.A., used under license. Trademarks indicated with ® are registered in the United States Patent and Trademark Office, the Canadian Trade Marks Office and in other countries.

Visit us at www.romance.net

Printed in U.S.A.

Books by Jodi O'Donnell

Silhouette Romance

Still Sweet on Him #969
The Farmer Takes a Wife #992
A Man To Remember #1021
Daddy Was a Cowboy #1080
Real Marriage Material #1213
Dr. Dad to the Rescue #1385

Silhouette Special Edition

Of Texas Ladies, Cowboys...and Babies #1045

JODI O'DONNELL

grew up one of fourteen children in small-town Iowa. As a result, she loves to explore in her writing how family relationships influence who and why we love as we do.

A *USA Today* bestselling author, Jodi has also been a finalist for the Romance Writers of America's RITA Award and is a past winner of RWA's Golden Heart Award. She lives in Iowa with her two dogs, Rio and Leia.

Dear Sam,

We haven't been communicating too well lately, have we, son? So I thought maybe a letter would help me get out some things I don't seem able to say. The fact is, I'm at a loss as to what to do, and it isn't a feeling I'm used to.

I know it's been a rough year since your mother died. Rough for us both. And what with being so busy moving us to Dallas and getting established here as an ER doctor, I haven't always been there for you. I don't have much of an excuse for that, except to say I'm doing my best. You see, I lost both my parents when I wasn't much older than you are now. Lost them—and my best friend in the whole world, Elsa Dog.

I know you miss your mother, Sam. Believe me when I say I'd give anything to bring her back. But I can't, so we'll have to go on without her. We still have each other, you know, even if it seems to me you could use a friend.

Maybe we both could use a friend. Someone faithful and loyal and true. Someone whose love and devotion would help you heal and believe in the future again. Someone like E.D. was to me. But I also need something—*someone*—more. And it would take a miracle....

Love, Dad

Prologue

Rural East Texas, twenty-four years ago

Pale legs flashed between breaks in the brush as the boy raced headlong through the pine woods. His jagged breathing was the only sound in the early-evening silence.

Matching her gait to his, as she did everything, the golden retriever loped alongside him, worry in the brown-eyed glances she cast up at him.

Lungs bursting and heart about to, Holden McKee collapsed on the cushioned ground, soaked from days of April rains. Even now the downpour started again, drops pattering down between the thick canopy of evergreen boughs.

Holden didn't care that the damp seeped into the seat of his cutoffs as he sucked in air and the scent of loamy earth, pine resin and silty river water.

He swallowed, trying as he'd been trying for weeks not to break down. He was ten years old. Too big to blubber like a baby.

But his mother was dying!

The retriever's tongue swiped at his cheek, taking away raindrops and the few tears that escaped from Holden, despite his efforts.

"Cut it out, E.D.," he scolded not very strongly, fending off the dog's advances. He gave the retriever a smile to show he didn't mean it. Her chestnut eyes showed sympathy. She cleaned another swatch of his cheek, and he *was* comforted, as always, by her loyalty. Sometimes it seemed she was the only one who understood him.

He didn't know what he'd do without her.

Holden buried his face in the dog's neck. "Oh, Elsa Dog."

She'd been his friend and companion for five years, ever since the pup had been given to Holden's father when he'd refused to take payment from a patient he knew struggled to keep food on his family's table. That was Samuel McKee's way, putting others' concerns before his own. Just like two winters ago when a bad flu outbreak hit the county, and he'd seen to everyone's health before his own. His mercy had cost him his life.

And now...now God was calling home Holden's mother, too.

"So what's going to happen to *me?*" Holden muttered rebelliously into Elsa's ear. He'd done pretty well so far, keeping faith that things would turn out somehow. But right now he couldn't find it in him to trust God knew his business.

Elsa whimpered softly, probably because of the tight grip he had around her. He didn't ease up but clasped her tighter to him.

The retriever leaned into him, solid and true. Her copper-and-gold coat glowed like a halo. How could someone not want such a pretty dog?

Blinking back more tears, Holden tried to distract himself by staring up through the trees. It did the trick, for he noticed two pines standing side by side, both with forks in their trunks, which was unusual enough, but the top of one split trunk crossed over the other.

"X" marks the spot, he thought. Like in a treasure hunt. And this was his spot, his very own corner of the world. He belonged *here,* not in some strange house in the suburbs of a city, away from all that was familiar and dear.

Holden set his jaw. "I won't go. No way they can make me." And no way would he leave without Elsa.

Holden launched himself to his feet and continued into the woods toward the river and the section of undercut bank he'd come to think of as his.

Within minutes, though, Holden was up to his ankles in freezing mud. Wiping the raindrops from his eyes with one sleeve of his sodden T-shirt, he peered through the undergrowth. It looked like the path to his hideout might be underwater. Should he turn back?

But there was something he kept wedged in a cranny in that hideout. Secured in a watertight box were his most treasured possessions.

He *couldn't* lose everything he cared about all at once.

Holden gritted his teeth against the lump that rose in his throat, thinking about how his mother had called him to her bedside this afternoon and told him that Aunt Tina and Uncle Dwight would take care of him from now on; Chicago would be his new home. Would he try, for her, to be good—to be happy?

Holden had wanted to reassure her. But he couldn't speak, or he'd have poured out his fear and heartbreak to her. Still, she'd known.

Then she'd laid her hand on his cheek and gazed down at him with tear-filled eyes, and he'd sensed she wasn't able to find the courage to tell him something else. But what could be worse than losing your mother and having to leave your home forever?

When he'd come out of Mama's bedroom, Elsa had risen

from her spot by the door, and he'd noticed the look in his aunt's and uncle's eyes. They didn't have a large house, Aunt Tina said, and not much more than a patch of a yard. Cousin Seth, with whom Holden would be sharing a bedroom, had allergies....

Holden had gotten the message, loud and clear. That was when it had all seemed too much, too unfair. He tore out the door, Elsa at his heels and his mother's plea swept from his head.

His attention was brought abruptly back to the present as Holden found himself fighting for every foothold in water that had deepened to thigh-high. This was too dangerous, he scolded himself. He knew East Texas weather, knew better than to venture into rushing water.

And he knew he must go back. He couldn't let Mama down.

Something bumped up against the back of his knees, nearly upsetting his shaky footing. Elsa had already lost contact with the ground. Her front legs churned against the swelling current. Holden's hand shot out to secure her by her collar. He had to get them both out of there, fast.

"C'mon, girl. I won't let you drown."

Panting, Elsa gazed up at him in perfect trust.

He retraced their route, using the trunks of trees to pull himself along. He didn't dare let go of Elsa.

Finally, grimy with mud, bits of leaves and sticks clinging to his clothes and Elsa's coat, they made it to higher ground and the dog bounded up the incline ahead of him, shaking herself furiously. She turned and crouched in her usual playful stance—front legs spread wide as she went down on her elbows, hind end high in the air, a grin wreathing her face. Holden had to grin himself. Yes, the danger was over, for now.

Reaching up, he grabbed a low hanging branch to haul himself up that last stretch of the embankment. His hand closed over not rough bark but muscled smoothness, cold and wet and slimy—

A musky, rotting smell invaded his nose. Holden came eye to eye with a deadly cottonmouth.

Every hair on his body stood on end. He jumped away, but the ground was slippery and his feet flew out from under him. Tumbling backward, he came down in three-foot-deep water, going completely under. Yet within an instant, he was up and splashing, scrambling back however he could, arms flailing, his every effort aimed at putting as much distance between himself and sure death. Elsa would take care of herself, he knew. The retriever had been snake-proofed by his father, had had the lesson to avoid all reptiles drilled into her.

Except there was no getting away from a riled-up cottonmouth. Quick as lightning, it uncoiled from the tree branch and dropped to the ground before slithering toward Holden.

He could only backpedal deeper into the water, where he knew he'd have even less of a chance against the cottonmouth. His only hope was to find a long stick to catch the snake under its middle and fling it far away.

He was frantically feeling under the murky water for such a weapon when Holden heard a low growl. He spun. Terror sliced a trail straight up his spine, for Elsa's manner was now anything but playful as she squared off in front of the cottonmouth, directly between it and her master.

"Elsa!" he shouted, taking a step toward them. The current tugged at him. Had it grown that much stronger in just a few minutes? "Elsa, no!"

She retreated not one inch as, lips curled back, she bared sharp white teeth that would have made a lesser beast think twice about tangling with her.

Not the cottonmouth. Holden saw the snake rear up its triangular black head and open its jaws.

Hackles raised, the retriever raked the dirt with one paw, feigning first strike. Her water-soaked coat looked like polished copper, smooth as armor. Yet it wasn't armor; she was just a dog, with skin as tender as his.

"Elsa, *no!*" Holden yelled again, clambering out of the water, hoping to distract one or the other.

Then the snake struck, and in an endless moment all he could see were flashes of red-gold and the writhing, dark-brown whip of the reptile. The struggle propelled both dog and snake into the water, where Elsa completely submerged while still going after the cottonmouth for all she was worth. His heart pumping, Holden's eyes stung at the raw, fierce beauty of her.

Oh, his brave, loyal girl!

Just as suddenly it was over, the cottonmouth swimming away, oozing dark blood in its wake.

Had Elsa been bitten, too? Caring nothing for his own safety, Holden plunged once more into the floodwaters. But the flow *had* picked up, and he found himself being carried along. He'd have welcomed the current if it would bring him closer to Elsa, but she was moving as rapidly.

He should never have come here and tried to retrieve his treasure box! It wasn't worth losing Elsa.

He used his arms and legs as rudders to steer him toward the dog. He came within an arm's length of her, and Holden stretched out his hand as she thrashed toward him. His fingers caught a handful of slick fur—

Slam! He crashed into a tree trunk, which nearly knocked the wind out of him—and caused him to lose his hold on Elsa.

Holden wrapped his arms around the tree as he searched for the retriever. His heart sank when he located her. She was so very, very far away. If he let go of the tree trunk, he might never catch up to her and would surely lose his life.

It seemed hopeless.

"No!" Holden screamed. "Don't give up, Elsa!"

But he saw her losing strength, going under, then surfacing briefly, water spraying from her nostrils, chin stretched and straining. Her movements grew sluggish, weaker.

"Come *on*, girl," he pleaded. "Don't give up on me now!"

Her brown eyes fixed on him, valiant, devoted, loyal to the last. She blinked.

Then she was gone.

"Elsa! *Elsa!*"

He cried her name over and over, was whispering it hoarsely when Dwight and half the county found him hours later still clinging to that tree trunk, even though the water had receded.

They wrapped him in blankets, but the shivering didn't stop. He didn't think it ever would, and right then he didn't care.

Dwight pried the story out of him. Strangely, his uncle wasn't angry that Holden had risked his life over a dog. He set a forearm across Holden's shoulders and gave them a squeeze.

"She's gone, son," he said. Whether he meant Mama or Elsa wasn't clear.

Holden hunched his back in resistance and denial. But he couldn't hold back the truth: He had no one now. No one.

With a sob, he pressed his face against his uncle's side and cried for all he had loved and lost this day. He cared nothing for the treasure left in the cubbyhole on the edge of the river. That river had taken from him something much more precious. God had taken from him something much more precious.

And he would never, ever forget.

Leaning back in his heavenly throne, God gave a heavy sigh, anguished as always by his children's pain. Right now, Samuel McKee was waiting at the pearly gates for the arrival of his soul mate. Yet here was another soul who stood aching and alone.

It was not the boy's time, though. Holden McKee still had much work to do before he would be called home. It was why his canine companion had been placed there, to save the boy. And why God had given man such a creature—to bring the human spirit the example of unwavering trust and hopefulness and faith, which he wished for all his children to find.

"But how to bring them to such trust?" he mused. "Its promise is made on Earth every day—in the bloom of the rose, the rising of the sun, the birth of a child..."

Great fingers drummed a low rumble like thunder on the celestial armrest for a long moment, yet only a blink in time. Then his eyebrows parted like the clouds; eyes cleared like the dawn breaking.

"Of course!" he said. "How else on Earth can you glimpse a little bit of heaven?"

He peered lovingly down upon the boy Holden McKee as he was led home in the darkness.

"Have faith, my son," God whispered. "I have not forsaken you. In good time, the answers you seek will be yours."

Chapter One

Dallas, Texas, present day

There came a time in every little boy's life, Holden supposed, when he was forced to accept the inevitable and often painful fact that the ability to fly was reserved for birds, airplanes, comic book heroes—and certain "illusionists" who performed this amazing deed on prime-time television.

How often had Holden himself listened to such tales of disenchantment as he'd set collarbone or leg, stitched a split lip or patched up the odd contusion sustained as a result of some young man's literal leap of faith?

Telling himself this instance was no different, Holden shot a sidelong glance at his son, who sat next to him in treatment room three at the Brookside Physical Therapy Associates. Sam's face was pinched and pensive. Stoop-shouldered, the six-year-old cradled his splinted forearm against him as if protecting a newborn.

Somehow, Holden was not convinced.

Too bad the cast had had to come off this morning, just

when Sam seemed to be getting used to it. But there was still a lot of healing on his broken arm that needed to be done outside of such a protective shell.

"Are you having any pain?" he asked the boy.

Lips thinning, Sam shook his head.

Holden shifted in his seat, stretching an arm along the back of the empty chair on the other side of him. "That's good. You should have little discomfort, actually. You heard the orthopedist say the X ray showed the bones had realigned perfectly, didn't you?"

"Yes, sir."

He reached into his suit coat pocket. "You could put on some more of this lotion if your skin itches."

"I'm okay."

Holden felt his own mouth crease. He would have asked Sam what was the matter, what he *could* do for the boy, but he didn't think Sam would tell him. Ever since Sam's accident, the gap between father and son had grown, especially after Holden had tried to impress upon him the folly of allowing make-believe to take precedence over common sense.

He simply didn't know what to do or say or ask next, and had told the grief counselor Sam had been seeing just that. The man had given him the rather simplistic advice that Holden should let Sam make the next move. So far, his son had done nothing.

And so the gap widened, imperceptibly.

Yet what if Sam came to him with a question Holden couldn't answer, a problem he couldn't fix?

I'm scared.

And I miss her so much.

With a sigh, Holden dropped his chin and massaged a persistent and painful knot in his jaw muscle. He'd always had a tendency to clench his teeth when under stress, but if he didn't ease up soon, he'd crack every molar in his mouth.

"Dad?"

Holden lifted his head. "Yes?"

"I just wondered if—" Sam was looking at him anxiously. Not often did the boy see him showing any sign of vulnerability. After all he'd been through, Holden made sure of that.

He straightened his spine and asked again, "Yes?"

Sam's gaze slid away. "If I could, you know, hit the bathroom before the therapist comes in."

"Oh. Sure. I saw one when we came in. Down the hallway."

Resisting the urge to offer help, he watched the boy disappear, the door swishing shut behind him. Left alone, Holden let his head fall back against the wall behind him with an oath of self-censure. He really needed to pull himself together, once and for all, for Sam's sake, if nothing else.

But things had gotten so complicated, so close, lately.

He stared at the recessed spotlights above him and wondered if their brutal illumination, so like the flash-bulb brilliant lighting in the ER, might help him find the distance he usually donned as easily as a stethoscope. At least pondering the subject gave him something to concentrate on, take his mind off of…things.

Like how hard he'd been working. He'd thought leaving the job at County Hospital in Chicago and the daily dose of senseless death would help put his life on a more even footing. Yet even within the less-intensive atmosphere of a private suburban hospital, he continued to feel as if he slogged through a mire as thick as quicksand.

Holden realized the lights had burned hot spots on his retina only after he heard someone say his name. All he could see was a reddened aura surrounding the figure before him.

He closed his eyes, giving them a second to recover.

"Holden McKee?" the still faceless woman repeated. There was something strangely soothing about her voice. Yet rather than calming him, Holden recognized trepidation mingling with the sense of powerlessness he'd been fighting.

"Yes, I'm Holden McKee," he said blindly, not liking the sensation. "Who are you?"

"I'm here to help your son," she answered. She had a faint drawl he found rather attractive. "You, too, it would seem. Are you all right?"

"Yes, of course. It's just temporary. Stupid of me, looking into the light like that—"

A hand rested on his shoulder, delicate as an angel's touch. The impression was reinforced by the caress on the back of his hand, which felt like nothing so much as a feather.

With a certain urgency, Holden blinked. What finally came into focus was a young woman bending toward him, her face inches from his. He realized where he'd gotten the impression of auras and feather-light touches: she was surrounded by a glorious veil of red-gold hair, wavy and as fluid-looking as molten copper. The ends of its waist-length strands brushed his hand as it lay on his knee.

He got the strongest urge to reach up and rub a lock of it between his fingers to see if it was real. Or to bury his face in that thick curtain of softness—to see if she was real.

She smiled. "You look like you've seen a ghost."

"I don't believe in—"

The rest of his thought was lost as he was captured by a pair of fine brown eyes fringed with dark eyelashes so curly they curved right up over her brow bone. They were quite expressive—open and honest and caring. Quite...familiar.

With that realization, the calm Holden sought settled over him, as if now that the moment of reckoning was near, he could face it—wanted to face it—and get it over with, once and for all.

Her eyes darkened with bewilderment. He must be staring like a madman. His gaze faltered, bringing her mouth into his line of vision.

He found himself riveted by those full lips, so close to his. A mere heartbeat away. All it would take was the slightest shift in his position to bridge the gap between them in a kiss. And with that connection, somehow he would know...what?

The moment held, a wrinkle in time. He felt himself at a crossroads, as if he was being given a rare, brief glimpse of two possible paths to take.

Neither way was quite clear. So close, though.

"What did you say your name was?" Holden whispered, so elusive was the moment.

"It's Edie. Edie Turner." Her voice held puzzlement. She didn't know *him*, obviously. Disappointment mushroomed and spread in him.

The moment began to slip away.

Desperately, Holden riffled through a mental Rolodex for her name. *Edie Turner*. It struck no chords with him, but then he came into contact with so many people. Patients, colleagues, co-workers—all passed in and out of his life at such a rate they seemed one faceless blur. He had no time to stop and look closely at anyone, as he was doing now.

Close. So close.

Where on earth—and when—would he have known a woman named...Edie?

"You're late." The words popped out of Holden's mouth of their own volition. *Much too late*, he wanted to add.

At his accusing tone, she straightened in surprise. Her hand dropped away. "Yes, I-I am, I guess. A little. But we still have plenty of time. There'll be no one else after you."

Why did her assurance—and the hurt in her eyes—do nothing to soothe his sudden anger? In fact, that look nearly undid him again, especially coming on the heels of a moment when he'd almost felt he could have told this woman anything and she would have understood.

Unsure why he was so irritated, Holden stood and indicated the time on his watch. "My son's appointment was at four. It's now twenty after. That's more than a little late."

She took a step back. Whatever connection he'd felt between them snapped.

"I apologize for any inconvenience I've caused," she said, which only rankled him further.

"I just need to know if this is what I should expect when I bring Sam to his appointments. Because I can certainly put that twenty minutes to good use."

Edie gave the clipboard in her hand a quick glance. "It's *Dr.* McKee, isn't it?" she asked.

"Yes."

"Of course. Well—again—I apologize for the wait, Dr. McKee, but in the interest of providing the best treatment possible to our patients, appointments sometimes do run over." Though her tone remained polite, she flicked a long lock of that hair behind her shoulder in a telling gesture. "As a healthcare professional yourself, I'm sure you understand."

He raised an eyebrow at such insubordination. *Not* the wisest move on her part, but then—

"I deserved that, didn't I?" Holden said.

"You're the doctor." She returned his scrutiny steadily. She had spirit, he'd give her that.

Yet there was not a bit of recognition in her eyes for him. The caring warmth he'd spied there had definitely departed—if he'd actually seen it at all.

He shook his head. He really had been working too hard.

Holden massaged the back of his neck. "I'm the one who should apologize, Ms. Turner. I've been under a lot of strain, though that's hardly an excuse. I guess I don't blame you, getting back a bit of your own from a doctor. We're the ones who make the world wait for and on us," he quipped, trying for a lighter tone.

She seemed slightly mollified, enough to return mildly, "I think they call it a God complex, Dr. McKee."

Again, the words spilled out of his mouth of their own accord. "Not this doctor, Ms. Turner," he said with grim emphasis. "Because that would mean I believed there's such a thing as an almighty and healing God. And the fact is, we're on our own down here."

There was a muffled sound from behind him. Holden turned to find Sam had returned and stood in the doorway. He looked as if he'd learned there was no Santa Claus. Holden supposed, in a way, the boy had just endured a similar disillusionment.

His heart sank like lead.

"Sam, I—" Holden extended a hand toward the boy, then dropped it—and shut up. Just as before, he couldn't think of a single thing he could say to make the situation better. He *would* have given anything to take back his words. That he couldn't shake his bitterness about the turn their lives had taken was one thing, but his son ought to have some hope to sustain him.

Yet the futility of trying to make sense of such a loss was a strong force in Holden. Not for the first time, he wondered how he was going to raise this child, given his cynical view of life. Maybe that's what made him feel so world-weary. There were a thousand hurts he could heal, but what was that power if he couldn't heal the human spirit? Because his was next to lost. The dearth of hope and trust in him seemed so deep a debt, it would take a miracle to replenish it.

Edie had never seen a person look more forsaken, like he'd just lost his best friend.

The little boy stood in the doorway cradling his injured forearm, the faded-to-gray color of his jeans shorts echoed in eyes so like his father's. He held the support crossed on his chest, fist on his heart, as if he were set to swear an allegiance and waited only for someone to tell him to whom. And if no one did, he'd bolt at any moment.

In that instant, he owned her heart.

All the cautions given her by the clinic supervisor not three hours ago—that she could not be the world's rescuer and continue to work in health care—flew right out of Edie's head. How could she not respond to such a silent cry for help?

He was a handsome child, with those enormous eyes and that spiky dark-brown hair begging for a hand to smooth it down. She wondered what his mother was like, and what kept her from being here in her child's time of need.

Her heart squeezed painfully.

Edie tossed a reproachful glance at his father, whose own eyes—more gray-green than strictly gray—looked as bleak, his face carved from stone. Thank God he'd checked his tongue before completely demoralizing the boy. Even she had flinched at the gloom and doom in his voice. At least he seemed to perceive his blunder, for she saw the doctor's jaw bulge with the gritting of his teeth.

Reluctant sympathy stirred in her. She'd give him credit for his remorse, even if she had a feeling the damage had already been done, in so many ways.

She'd have to do the best she could with what was left.

"So you're Sam," Edie said, bending at the waist so she was on a level with the boy. Her action worked. Sam shifted his gaze from his father to her.

Edie smiled her warmest smile. "I'm Edie Turner, your physical therapist, which means I'm going to see if we can make that arm of yours better so you can get back to playing all your games. Why don't you hop up here on the table and we'll take a look at your arm?"

Sam complied, his climb-up made awkward by his continued grip on the white plastic splint. The padded surface sighed as he stoically settled on the edge of the plinth in front of her, sneaker-clad feet dangling. Yet when Edie moved to take a cursory look at his forearm, he recoiled.

She knew immediately to drop her hand. This would take some delicate maneuvering. Perhaps it would be best to get more acquainted first.

Edie pulled a pen from the pocket of her lab coat, flipping

to the history portion of Sam's file. "How'd you injure your arm, Sam?"

"He took a fall from the top of the stairs to the landing," the doctor interjected from behind her.

Edie turned to find him a few feet away in a rather commanding stance, with fists thrust into the pockets of his trousers, coattail flipped back behind him. He nodded toward Sam. "His injury involved a bone forearm fracture, completely displaced and the fragments overriding, which required closed reduction of Sam's arm and eight weeks' immobilization. Because of the nature of the fracture, the orthopedic surgeon decided to err on side of caution and recommended therapy."

He spoke to her as he would a class of first-year medical students, and with the same patronizing delivery.

Edie stifled a sigh. On the whole, the physicians she knew were a pleasure to work with. Yet despite his assertion to the contrary, Dr. Holden McKee seemed to be in firm possession of a power complex, divine or otherwise. Would it have killed him to drop the doctor-in-charge act and go stand near his son, give him a little moral support?

"So you accidently fell, Sam?" Edie pointedly asked the boy.

"Not 'xactly," he admitted. "I didn't fall. I sorta...jumped. I-I was trying to fly. You know, like David Copperfield."

"Aha. I guess that's where the landing part comes in. Not so smooth, was it, Sam?"

To her delight, Sam gave one of those deprecating, all-in-a-day's-hard-play shrugs.

She chuckled. "So I'd say it wasn't exactly a fall, wouldn't you?"

"I guess." He looked at his father over her shoulder. "I mean, no, ma'am. I didn't fly, I just fell."

"Oh, please call me Edie, will you?" She drew Sam's attention back to her with her request. "I want to be really comfortable with you."

"Okay—Ee-dee," he said, enunciating each syllable.

"Thanks. I appreciate it. So, how many steps were you aiming to soar over?" Nonchalantly, she reached out and adjusted one of the Velcro straps on the splint. "Five, six...more?"

"Eight," Sam owned. He threw another glance, this one guilty, over her shoulder.

"Eight!" she exclaimed, cocking her head to the right and into his line of vision. "I bet there must've been at least a second or two when you really did feel like you *were* flying."

He blinked at her. "Yeah, I guess I did."

Edie felt encouraged enough to ask, "Think I could have a look at the souvenir of such a feat?"

"Well...okay."

This time when she reached to remove the molded plastic splint, Sam allowed her to undo the straps and set it aside. His forearm and wrist were pale and somewhat atrophied from their weeks in plaster, yet looked to have healed well, with only a slight thickening still present.

Sam swallowed and averted his gaze. He seemed almost repelled by the sight of his own frailty.

"Why, you're mending just fine, Sam," she reassured him.

He squinted one eye. "Really?" he asked suspiciously.

"Yes, of course. Did you think you wouldn't?"

He gave another shrug of his small shoulders, but there was nothing devil-may-care about this one. "I-I guess I didn't know."

Once more, Edie felt her heartstrings wrench as she realized he'd been protecting his injury not just from her sight. The worry he must have been going through! Apparently he hadn't felt he could ask his father, the doctor, for an assessment—and an assurance.

The man wasn't exactly increasing in her estimation.

"Well, you *are* getting better, champ," she said. "We just need to keep up the good work that's already been done."

With infinite gentleness, Edie took Sam's forearm in her hands. But even that merest touch made the youngster flinch.

She felt another twist of her heart. He was obviously terrified. "I'm sorry, Sam. Does it feel uncomfortable just touching it?"

"Naturally he'll have some tenderness, with or without moving his arm, because of the nature of his injury," his father again broke in, finally stepping around to the other side of the examining table, next to his son. Yet he was as stiff as ever as he placed his hand on the brown leatherette surface next to Sam's hip, then seemed to recall himself and withdrew it.

She began to wonder if anything could penetrate that impassive shell of his.

He cleared his throat. "But it's important to begin moving the joint at this point so that its range of motion isn't permanently restricted and full function is recovered as soon as possible."

Edie wondered if this particular explanation was for her benefit or his six-year-old son's. All right, this time she'd try acknowledging his input and work with it. "Could that be it, Sam? You know, not the soreness right now, but being kind of scared of how it might cause a little discomfort to move your arm?"

"I dunno. Maybe."

"Are you scared what *I* might do will cause discomfort, Sam?"

Chin tucked, he chewed his lip. Then he nodded. "A-a little." His voice trembled, the poor little boy.

The doctor made a sound, no doubt gearing up for what was sure to be another of his textbook interpretations of the problem, which would naturally be so helpful to Sam. Quickly, she shot Holden a forestalling glance, hoping this time he'd get the message. Normally, parents didn't involve themselves in their children's treatment once the therapist had established a rapport with the child. As a medical professional, Dr. McKee should know better than to interfere with that process, although she had a feeling getting him to give up even a little control to her was going to be an uphill battle.

She saw a muscle spasm pulse in his jaw. He inclined his head ever so slightly, yielding to her judgment. For now.

Edie turned her focus back to Sam, whose hunched shoulders had drawn up even more, until he looked like a turtle retreating into its shell.

He would break her heart before this was over, Edie was certain. Something told her what she did in the next few moments would make all the difference in the world to this boy.

"You know, Sam, it's all right to be scared." She made her voice very hushed, just between the two of them. "I won't lie to you and say what we're going to do won't feel a little uncomfortable for you, but we won't do anything you're not okay with. Deal?"

He didn't answer.

Oh, what to do with a boy who shut everyone out of his pain! Edie was at a loss for how to proceed, was acutely aware Dr. McKee watched her every move. The words of her supervisor rang in her brain. *You can't let yourself get so emotionally involved, Edie. It's not good for the patient—your judgment isn't as clear—and it's not good for you. You'll end up losing yourself, burning out.*

Yet every cell in her urged her not to hold back, and not just with Sam. Edie didn't know why, but something told her that by doing so even a little, she would lose a part of herself. If she stifled the emotion, then she stifled her ability to connect.

She'd become like the doctor here.

She found herself wondering again where Sam's mother was, could not imagine what kept her from being with him—and her husband.

On that thought, Edie laid her palm on Sam's shoulder—

much as she'd done moments earlier with Holden, it occurred to her. But it just seemed the thing to do, both then and now.

And such was the power of a simple touch that the boy responded like his father had. His head came up, chestnut-brown hair falling over his forehead, and he peered at her, gaze searching.

"Will you trust me, just a little, Sam?" she murmured.

Dark lashes flickered, as if he were afraid to believe in what she offered. But then, hadn't he stood there barely ten minutes ago and listened to his father insist upon the futility of believing in anything or anyone? Then to have that point driven home by being forced to admit he shouldn't have believed he could fly!

How many more hopes and dreams could this child stand to have dashed?

"Will you trust me, Sam?" Edie urged.

His brow furrowed—as if he were afraid *not* to believe.

You can believe in this, Sam, she telepathed to him. *My help, my understanding, my friendship. My allegiance.*

Sam nodded. "'Kay. I'll trust you."

Relief washed over her. So the damage *was* repairable at this point.

"I'm glad you've put your trust in me, Sam," she said around the lump in her throat. "I won't let you down."

With a smile of confidence, Edie glanced up at Holden.

Eyes hard as granite met hers.

"Is making personal affirmations to patients standard practice at this clinic, Ms. Turner?" he asked in that instructor-to-student manner.

Her face grew hot. She couldn't entirely blame him for that; by making her promise to Sam, *she* was the one who wasn't being entirely professional. Yet she couldn't find it in her to regret doing so. She'd had to follow her instincts.

"Do you think it better to tip the scale on the other end of the spectrum, Dr. McKee?" she asked, with that same air of them having a friendly debate, her calming hand still upon Sam's shoulder. "Detach yourself completely from another's distress when you have the ability to help ease it?"

"Of course not. But we're not miracle workers. Too much is out of your control, and what is could get yanked out from under you in an instant—"

He broke off, clearly angry at himself for losing some of *his* control. "All I'm saying is, don't make promises you can't keep, Ms. Turner."

Not to my son. She was well aware of his unspoken addendum, was well aware that Sam listened and might pick up on the tone of their conversation.

"But that's just it. I haven't." She lifted her chin. "I *will* help Sam to the very best of my ability, Dr. McKee. *You* may depend on that, too."

He studied her as skeptically as ever but said no more. Truly, she didn't want to butt heads with him—especially not in front of Sam—but she had to do what she thought best.

Settling that aim in her mind, Edie turned her complete attention back to the boy. "All right, then! Let's get an idea of what's going on with that arm. Can you try and make a fist for me, Sam?"

Though obliging enough, the loose fist Sam curled his fingers into seemed not altogether his best effort. True to form, Dr. McKee was Johnny-on-the-spot with a pithy piece of medical advice. "Simple flexion of the fingers doesn't significantly demonstrate range of elbow motion and forearm rotation."

Whether he meant the comment for her enlightenment or Sam's wasn't clear. She only saw the boy's mouth go taut.

She really was losing her patience.

"You know what I just realized?" Edie said. "That this trust thing sort of works both ways. Meaning we need to trust *you*, Sam, to be the judge of how much you can do. Don't you agree, Dr. McKee?" She gazed at him innocently.

Holden's own mouth went rigid as another of those spasms pulsed in his square jaw. "Of course," he answered.

"Great." She nodded to Sam. "Just give it your best shot, champ."

Tongue curled up over his lip, Sam made a fist not much tighter than the last. Regardless, Edie made sure her praise was lavish—and quick. "Very good! Now try touching your pointing finger to your thumb...now your middle finger, right...ring finger, then pinkie. There you go!"

The boy's shoulders relaxed visibly, she noted with satisfaction. "I guess...I guess maybe I will be able to play again. Regular stuff, I mean. Not magic tricks."

"Well, it is pretty hard learning you've got a long way to go to be a master illusionist—or an escape artist, like I wanted to be when I was about your age. I was going to be the next Harry Houdini. Squeeze my fingers, will you, Sam? Hard as you can, but don't hurt me, okay?"

Sam actually cracked a one-sided smile, even as he earnestly concentrated on complying with her request. The result seemed most promising. He was loosening up, both literally and figuratively. "Playing Harry Hou...who?"

"Harry Houdini. He was a very famous magician who specialized in escaping from things. Yup, I cracked my head a good one trying to escape from a straitjacket while hanging upside down."

The boy's eyes rounded. "Really?"

"'Course I didn't have a real straitjacket, just an old bedsheet I wrapped around myself after I'd shinnied up a tree. Lost my balance before I even got—"

"Ms. Turner."

Edie glanced up. She'd forgotten Holden was there. "Yes?"

The look on his face was impassive no more. *Forbidding* was more like it. "Sam doesn't need any more ideas on magic tricks. If you really must continue on that bent, you might encourage him to try some sleight of hand, like making a quarter disappear, which would not only mobilize his arm but keep him occupied with less-dangerous activities."

Imperceptibly, Sam drew his shoulders up.

That did it, Edie decided. She'd hoped to avoid a confrontation, but it seemed inevitable.

"Would you excuse me for a moment?" she said.

She left the room and returned a minute later with the perky young woman who was her aide.

"Colleen here is going to put some moist heat on your arm to help loosen it up, okay, Sam?"

She turned to Colleen. "Nothing too intense. Sam's real good about letting you know what he can stand."

"Got it," Colleen said.

Edie smiled politely at Holden, but her words brooked no dissent. "If you'll come with me, Dr. McKee, I need to consult with you a moment."

He raised one dark eyebrow. "I welcome the opportunity."

Oh, yeah, she was in for a fight.

Edie gave Sam a wink of reassurance. "You'll be fine, champ, I promise."

He nodded bravely. "Okay, Ee-dee."

She couldn't prevent herself from delivering a parting touch in the form of smoothing down that spiky hair. "You know, I kind of like the special way you say my name," she teased.

Her heart melted at the yearning that sprang to his eyes as a result of her gesture, even as he shied away from it.

"I-I never knew anybody with initials for a name," he said hesitantly. "What's E.D. short for, anyway?"

The question, so out of the blue, brought her up short.

"But it's not...that," she stammered, wondering why she felt as if she was equivocating. "It's *Edie*. I don't think it's short for anything. My mother told me the name came to her in a dream when she was pregnant."

For some reason, she found her gaze locking with Holden's. He was impassive no more—instead she glimpsed a naked yearning in his eyes that was startling. It brought to mind how he'd stared at her before, right after she'd come into the room and found him looking almost...lost. And how it seemed he looked to her to bring him back home.

Edie was held spellbound by the searching in those intense gray-green eyes. They delved miles deeper than Sam's ever could—almost intimately. Like a man would gaze at...at a lover.

She realized only now how she'd avoided that look before, much in the same way his little boy had recoiled from her and the potential for pain she represented.

With some desperation, Edie pushed such thoughts from her mind so that she might concentrate on helping the one who needed her most at the moment.

But she was not quite so confident as she'd been a minute ago of who that person was as she left the room, Holden McKee only a step behind her.

Chapter Two

Holden followed Edie down the hall, where she indicated he should precede her into an unoccupied treatment room. She closed the door after them, startling him when she whirled to face him. Gone was the gentle, compassionate angel of mercy, surrounded by her halo of red-gold hair, who had so recently ministered to his son.

In her place was a fierce, passionate champion outfitted in an armor of copper. Her brown eyes snapped, the color in her cheeks rose. She was magnificent to behold.

A surge of some force passed over Holden, through him, paralyzing him like an electrical shock. What *was* it about this woman that resounded in him so profoundly? Like that ripple in time he'd felt before, which he'd begun to believe had been a result of the stress he was under.

Yet it had happened again in the treatment room with Sam—that little misunderstanding about her name. That time, though, she'd experienced a jolt, too, which he'd seen disorient her.

It wasn't just him—or was it? He *had* been under a lot of

stress—the job, the move, this new crisis with Sam. The changes and events of the past year were simply catching up with him. That had to be it.

He could not succumb to the confusion.

"Let's get a few things straight right now, Dr. McKee," Edie began, starting right in on him, just as he knew she would. Well, he had a few things to say to her, too. "You've brought Sam to me for physical therapy. I am assuming this is because your ability to provide such treatment is outside your expertise. Am I wrong?"

"No, but—"

"Then why won't you let me do my job!" she demanded.

He crossed his arms, determined to remain calm and keep from taking her attack personally, even though she was stepping way out of line. Even though something told him he wasn't the only one taking things personally right now. "Precisely how have I prevented you, Ms. Turner?"

She stared at him with patent disbelief. "Are you serious? What do you call the lectures on this bone being connected to that bone so that I feel like I'm in Anatomy 101 again? But you know what? I can handle that. I've dealt with worse attacks on my competence by doctors. What's really damaging to any progress I might be making is your indirect criticism of just about anything Sam says or does!"

Holden was surprised into protesting, "Now, that is *not* true."

"Dr. McKee, please!" Clearly frustrated with him, she paced to the other side of the room, where she pivoted and slapped her palms down on top of the waist-high table. "He needs to tell me himself where it hurts and how it feels and what he's comfortable doing. You are not inside his body with him! Only Sam knows what he can tolerate. You should *know* that as a physician!"

"First of all, Ms. Turner, I did take your hints—as a physician—and kept my mouth shut while you worked at building a rapport with your patient so you could evaluate him," Holden said evenly, crossing to the table and planting his knuckles on it to face her squarely. "But I was forced to speak out at that last bit of yours, when you practically drew him a diagram of how to break his neck!"

"I was trying to let him know he hadn't done anything but be a typical little kid!" She leveled an accusing glare at him. "And don't tell me you're not angry with Sam for that."

Despite his resolution, Holden felt his control slip. "I am not angry! Why would I be when he's done nothing wrong?"

"Hasn't he? Launching himself down a staircase head-first?"

Holden's chin snapped back. Though the accident had happened over a month ago, the mere thought of that day had the power to propel him into a snare of self-blame he'd scarcely become untangled from.

Blast Edie Turner for making him go there!

"This sort of psychoanalyzing hardly falls within your function as Sam's therapist," he said through gritted teeth.

"I think it does! Sam's emotional state affects how well I can do my job, which is helping him to recover from his injury."

"Which I have my doubts of your being competent to do." Holden leaned forward on his fists. "I can have you taken off this case, and don't think I won't do it."

Now it was her turn to be taken aback. "You wouldn't be so rash at your son's expense."

"Would it be rash? I'm not convinced."

Edie blinked, her mouth working with frustration. But she rallied. "Certainly, you must do what you feel is best, Doctor. Which doesn't change the fact that Sam needs to hear from someone that sometimes kids *do* reckless and even kind of foolish things, like jumping off of landings and falling out of trees, and that such a mistake won't be held over his head forever. I mean, honestly, didn't you ever try some dangerous, foolish feat when you were a kid and nearly come to complete disaster?''

At her question, Holden took another hit, like a bomb going off inside him. Too close this time. Too damn close. The heat of it radiated around him.

This time he knew he'd be unable to temper his reaction, which only added more fuel to it.

"Of course I did!" he exploded, his face inches from hers. "Does that mean Sam's accident shouldn't have scared the hell out of me? Good God, Ms. Turner, I may be a doctor, but he's my son!"

His words reverberated in the room and seemed to bring both of them back to their senses. Holden rocked back on his heels, yanking one hand through his hair. He hated feeling out of control!

Yet his outburst had obviously struck a chord with Edie. Her fingers covered her open mouth as she gaped at him for several moments. She pressed one palm to her chest.

"You're right," she said simply. "I apologize, Dr. McKee. I haven't been dealing with you as a parent. As a...a person. I realize now your comments, however analytical or critical or inept, were your way of showing concern for your son."

"*So* glad you understand," Holden muttered, cramming his fists in his pockets.

She actually smiled, and it changed the whole aspect of her appearance, brought back that warmth of spirit she'd shown with Sam and less that role of fierce protector of all that was innocent—with Holden starring as the barbarian invader.

He even found himself adding ruefully, "I suppose I might have given you the impression I was treating Sam like any other case with my comments. I only meant to offer him encouragement."

His olive branch, such as it was, seemed to be accepted.

"Well, don't be too hard on yourself," Edie said. "I bet there were some of the usual father-son dynamics working there, too—you know, that male trait of not being able to be open with understanding or sympathy. Or maybe—" she cocked her head to one side, that fall of hair sliding down the length of her arm "—you've been angry with *yourself,* for letting him get hurt. Maybe that's what I was picking up on in the other room."

"'Picking up on'?" he asked cynically.

"Having Sam suffer an accident might be harder for a doctor to accept, even one who claims to have no power issues."

He felt himself tacking back toward ticked off at this woman. "Please, Ms. Turner, I really can do without the pop psychology. Which brings up a point." She wasn't the only one who could render a performance evaluation. "Speaking as a doctor now, you need to keep more of a professional distance and do your job. You're a physical therapist, not his shrink or his mother."

Her chin set rebelliously at his suggestion, but she answered readily enough. "Point taken, Doctor."

Holden had just begun to think he was getting a leg up on the situation—and Edie Turner—when she said, "Which brings up yet another matter. Where *is* Sam's mother?"

It was another blow to the gut, and it left him just a little more exposed than after the last.

This was why he avoided becoming personal with people.

"My wife died a little over a year ago," Holden said without a bit of inflection. Oh, but would the words ever get any easier?

At least they had the effect of stunning Edie into another silence, except for a murmured "I see."

The silence drew on, making Holden search to fill it with something, anything to draw them away from the dangerous ground he seemed to step onto with this woman with regularity.

"Now you know what Sam's dealing with," he said stiffly.

"Yes," she said on an outrush of air. "Knowing of your

loss certainly clears a lot of things up for me. At least I understand a little better the rather...pessimistic philosophy you let fly with earlier."

"Sure, I'm pessimistic," he said. "Can you make rhyme or reason out of why a woman in her prime might be struck down with a brain aneurysm?"

"I don't know why. That doesn't mean there isn't a reason."

Before he could react to such an absurd remark she'd gone on with infinite gentleness, "I'm...terribly sorry, Dr. McKee. For both yours and Sam's loss."

"Sorry?" Holden asked. "It's not your fault."

"Neither is it yours," she answered as gently, not rising to his gibe. Her brown eyes no longer snapped with righteousness. On the contrary, within their liquid depths were echoes of the sympathy and understanding he'd seen there before, when she'd leaned over him, her face—her mouth—so close to his he had almost kissed her.

At least now that temptation was held at bay by the treatment table that separated them like two adversaries. Except...Edie's hand lifted from the table. Holden watched, nearly mesmerized, as she held it out toward him, a lock of that vibrant hair caught on her cuff. It fanned down from her sleeve to her lab coat in a curtain of burnished copper.

If she touched him, he wasn't certain what he'd do.

Yes, exposed was exactly how he felt. Exposed and not in control at all.

But Edie apparently thought better of the gesture, for she let her hand drop to her side. Holden cleared his throat, wondering what had held her back.

She drew in a deep breath, looking somewhat troubled. "Well, then, Dr. McKee. Are we agreed that the most important thing is Sam's welfare?"

"Of course."

"And what's best, I think, is for me to gain his confidence

and trust." She stuck her hands into the pockets of her lab coat. "Most of all, I need to be able to work on his PT at a pace he's comfortable with, preferably in an atmosphere where his efforts aren't explicitly or implicitly judged."

Holden lifted a cool eyebrow. "Meaning?"

"You want him to come out of this with a fully rehabilitated forearm and wrist, and without any lingering fears about his injury, don't you?"

"Of course I do."

"Then I'd like you to let me treat Sam—without you."

His other eyebrow shot up.

Her gaze became determined. "I'm sure you're well aware giving PT to a child outside of a parent's presence is normal procedure. In fact, most parents feel it's easier on their nerves as well their child's."

"And if I don't hold that opinion?"

"You could ask for another therapist. I'm asking you not to do that." Her gaze turned almost pleading now. "Please. Let me help Sam."

Indeed, her brown eyes beseeched him. With a stifled oath, Holden turned, focusing on a chart of the human skeletal system tacked to the wall.

What was it about this woman that made him want to shake her one instant and the next take her in his arms?

She didn't see him as a parent—or even as a person! Well, appearances aside, Holden thought sarcastically, he was both. But he was also a doctor, and perhaps that was what she'd been getting at—that he closed himself within that persona to keep from letting emotion cloud his judgment. Often, it was this very ability to disconnect that permitted him to give a patient the best care. But Sam was not a patient; Sam was his son. And because he was, Holden felt all the normal feelings of fear and guilt and anger.

Nevertheless, he couldn't help but believe that he still must continue to set those feelings aside—for Sam's sake, as she'd said.

No, on first pass, he didn't like her suggestion, but the second and third times around his head, he saw the sense in it. Whatever Edie Turner was, she was committed. Even passionate, in a way that perhaps was imprudent while still being completely reliable. In part, he was glad she was just so, for it did seem to be exactly what Sam needed, or she wouldn't have made such progress with him in the short time she'd worked with him.

Yet another part of him, Holden acknowledged, rued that very development. *He* wanted to help his son. But as much as he hated to admit it, he wasn't doing the boy any good the way he was now. Edie had the right idea: Sam's welfare *was* his main concern.

Holden turned back to her. "All right, Ms. Turner. I'll still be bringing Sam to his appointments, and you can call me in toward the end of each session to show me the exercises he'll be doing. He'll need my help to do them right, and I want to be there for him. I do promise not to push him or make him feel like he's damaged himself in my eyes in any way. Fair enough?"

Relief broke out over her face as she smiled. "Fair enough."

He held the door for her as Edie led the way back to the treatment room where Sam was. She paused outside the door, though, and looked up at him.

"Thank you, Dr. McKee, for seeing the sense in my suggestion." She made a graceful swaying gesture with her head that swung her hair back over her shoulder. It really was her best feature, Holden decided. "I appreciate you putting your trust in me."

She'd made the same statement to Sam, and despite still questioning the wisdom of such an assurance, Holden found himself liking that she'd make the same one to him, too. It occurred to him then that she might be apprehensive about what had happened back in the other treatment room.

"Just so you know, I won't switch Sam to another therapist once he's started with you," he said gruffly. "You have my word."

"I trust you, Dr. McKee," she said, eyes vibrant with that emotion, undoubtedly sincere.

He would wonder later what impulse made him reach out and take a lock of that living mantle in his fingers. Edie stiffened but didn't pull away, emboldening him to leisurely rub the strands between thumb and forefinger. Each filament was like that of a precious metal, shimmering in the light. And soft, like the feathers he'd imagined he'd felt as the tips of these copper-gold locks had brushed the back of his hand. As then, it took all his might not to surround himself in the curtain of her hair.

"Is it really as easy as that, Edie?" he murmured. "You say you trust someone, so then you do? I give my consent, and so I've given you my trust? Is believing really that effortless?"

He waited for her answer, still caressing the silky strands. When none came, he glanced up. The trust had been replaced by the same disorientation he'd seen at Sam's misinterpreting her name.

"Naturally, it's not that easy," she said, her voice low. "Real trust can't be built in a day. It'll take time for Sam to put his faith in me. But I won't let your son down."

"Yes...Sam." Holden dropped the lock of hair and stepped back. "Shall we get back to him?"

As he followed Edie through the door, he realized that, indeed, like Rome, real trust could not be built in a day. Yet he knew from experience that it could burn to the ground in an instant.

He would have to be very careful—for everyone's sake.

* * *

Edie pushed open the door from the changing room to the pool area, her running shoes dangling from two fingers, her socks tucked under one arm. Warm, humid air surrounded her, along with the pervading smell of chlorine. Music continued to blast from a boom box on a bench, even though the seniors' hydrotherapy class had ended five minutes earlier. Several of the attendees were still tooling around in the pool on their foam boards.

She spied her aunt Hazel among the balding pates and bathing caps just as the older woman saw her.

"How'd it go today?" Edie called above the echoing strains of Brooks & Dunn's "Boot Scootin' Boogie."

"Fine." Hazel dog-paddled over. "This left hip of mine is acting up again. Fool thing."

"Hey there, Edie," called one of the older gentleman.

"'Lo, Ralph." She shoehorned her heel into her shoe with one finger and nodded toward Hazel. "Say, would it be possible for you to give her a lift in tomorrow afternoon, too, and I'll see if I can get a room where some work can be done on Hazel's hip?"

"You betcha."

Edie grinned at the sight of her aunt's pink cheeks. Ralph Janssen gave Hazel a ride to hydrotherapy class on Tuesdays and Thursdays, even though her house was out of his way, allowing Hazel to then ride back home with Edie. Ralph's motives were not altogether altruistic. It was obvious to everyone that he was sweet on Hazel, but the older woman would hear nothing about it.

"Actually," Edie suggested, "you wouldn't have to come in tomorrow—so long as you spend another twenty minutes bare minimum doing your stretching exercises in the water while I'm working out, okay?"

Hazel frowned at her mightily. The pool was Ralph's element. He could hang out there forever.

"Hey, Edie, whyn't you join us?" Ralph asked.

Edie concentrated on picking a knot out of her shoelace. On a shrug, she answered, "I'm not much of a water person, to tell the truth. I guess it's from growing up near Lubbock where the most water a person sees at one particular time is at the bottom of their bathtub—and that's only during the wet season."

Ralph laughed. "I thought I heard a West Texas twang. What brings a small-town girl like you all the way to Dallas?"

Instantly, the answer popped into her head: *Holden McKee*. If her mouth had been open, she'd have said it. Holden McKee.

A premonition rippled through her, making her shiver in the warm, humid air.

"You know why, Ralph," Hazel jumped in. "She's my caretaker. Gave up a good job in Lubbock to come be with me. Without her, I'd be in a nursing home." She gave an emphatic nod. "Yup, she's been nigh onto a savior to me."

Edie smiled at her aunt with great affection. Rheumatoid arthritis certainly limited Hazel's activity, but she was hardly an invalid. If anything, the older woman inspired Edie, for Hazel Turner lived daily with pain that was literally bone deep. Yet her spirit would not allow her to sink into despair. Whatever her limits, she lived life to the very edge of them, fearlessly so.

As for being a savior, it was Hazel who'd been one to Edie, urging her six months ago to leave Lubbock behind and come live with her. Family should be with family, her aunt had said, and each was all the family either had left.

"Thanks for the vote of confidence, Aunt Hazel, but flattery goes as far with me as it does with you." Setting her hands on her thighs and shoving off, Edie stood and pointed a finger at her aunt. "Stretches. Twenty minutes. I mean it."

"Oh, all right," Hazel said.

Edie was still chuckling a minute later as she programmed the treadmill. She'd have preferred an outdoor run, but her hours rarely permitted it. At least at this time of the evening she had the equipment in the exercise room to herself. And she had Hazel's company on the rather long commute home to rural Parker.

She sank into an easy rhythm, her mind coasting as impressions of her day sifted into place, such as the high school athlete with a torn rotator cuff she was rehabilitating, her conversation with the clinic supervisor…

Then there was Holden McKee. Of its own volition, her mind called up a picture of father and son, with their expressive eyes—one set gray, like beaten pewter, the other the gray-green of verdigris—and that unruly chestnut brown hair that both contended with.

Of course. She must have been thinking of Holden's son when Ralph had asked what brought her to Dallas. Not that Sam *had* brought her here. It had been more like a sense of real purpose that had infused her upon seeing him. The serious, dark-haired boy had tugged good and strong on her heartstrings. She didn't get many children that young as patients; they were open books, their struggles written clearly on their faces. Naturally he'd make an impression on her.

But no denying it, there'd also been the tug from Sam's father, perhaps because she was quite grateful to him. Holden McKee could have demanded a different therapist for his son today, which surely would have led her supervisor to giving her a formal reprimand. At one point, Edie almost thought Holden *might* report her.

But he hadn't. He hadn't let ego or pride or whatever drove him get in the way of doing what was right for his son.

There may be hope for you yet, Holden McKee, she thought wryly as she upped her pace so that she was now at a fast jog.

Yes, one had to look harder and work harder to bring out the flashes of humanity within him, such as when his son had first entered the treatment room on the heels of his incriminating remark. Or when he'd burst out at her about fearing for his son.

Or when he'd first looked at her, gaze open and unguarded.

It had been the memory of that look that had compelled her to hold out her hand to him across the width of the table. The man lived in a world of pain, and while he couldn't be blamed for wanting to protect himself from more, neither could he remain in that place forever. Now seemed a particularly significant time for Holden McKee, when he might turn toward his son, toward the pain of losing his wife and get past it to heal.

Or he might just as easily turn away.

Edie didn't think she could stand by and watch that happen to Sam. Happen to both of them. Happen to all of them.

She frowned, shaking her head. Maybe her supervisor had a point. Maybe Edie did need to pull back, take a more objective stance. Not become so emotionally involved. She'd certainly felt uncomfortable with the closeness generated by Holden's own reaching out to her, capturing her hair in his fingers....

Thankfully, just then the pace on the treadmill kicked up to ten miles an hour—fast yet still well within Edie's capacity. But it did take more of her concentration.

She regulated her respiration, two strides breathing in, two strides breathing out. She felt her body straining for oxygen. Just a few more minutes and she'd be in the zone...

Legs churning. Hard arms thrashing through a thick fog. Heart pounding.

Edie drew in a gasp, upsetting her rhythm. What...?

Images flashed before her eyes: *Woods, all around. A boy. A dark-haired boy.*

What was happening?

With a note of alarm, Edie noticed that her breathing had suddenly become uneven, almost labored, as if she were afraid and trying to get away from something—or someone. She struggled to bring it back under control. Two in, two out.

Now there was shouting. He was shouting something at her. Screaming it. Very upset. "Don't...don't give..."

Edie's throat closed. She stumbled, caught herself with a hand on the side rail. Through a haze of emotion, she found the stop button and jabbed it.

The treadmill ground to a halt.

Her breathing came in gulps. Flattening her hand against her stomach, Edie tried to bring it back under control, her other hand clutching the rail for balance. She felt so dizzy, spinning around and around. She pressed two fingers to the side of her throat. Her heart was going like a trip-hammer.

Edie staggered over to one of the weight machines and sat down on its padded bench. She dropped her head between her knees, sucking air. What had happened? It had been as if she were inside someone else's head, in a whole different place. The dark-haired boy: could it be Sam? Had she picked up on something the child was feeling?

What was that poor little boy dealing with right now?

Edie sat up, fingers digging into her thighs. Was she already in too deep with this child? Because she realized she wanted to see Sam McKee very badly right then, wanted to hold him, comfort him, let him comfort her—

Almost as badly as she did not want to see his father.

With a shaking hand, Edie wiped the perspiration from her forehead. No. All this was about was her internalizing her perceptions about both Sam and Holden. Whatever it was, whatever scared her about Holden, she couldn't let it overcome her. Sam needed her. If she had to contend with certain feelings between his father and herself, then she would do it.

She would not be the first to turn away.

Chapter Three

"Can you try a royal wave for me now, Sam?" Edie said. "As if you're greeting your loyal subjects. Excellent! How about some Motown moves?" Hand on her hip, she stuck her arm out straight and cocked her wrist. "Like, 'Stop! In the Name of Love.'"

Grinning bashfully, the boy followed suit, earning him more kudos. Pride filled Edie's chest. Only three therapy sessions, and Sam was coming along splendidly. If anything, he seemed even more pleased than she, and Edie had to give credit for the boy's changed attitude to Dr. McKee. Even if Holden's manner toward her was strained at best, he'd obviously been true to his word in setting aside his own emotional issues in order to see to Sam's.

Whatever he was doing seemed to be working. Sam's handsome face took on a look of amazement at being able to extend his wrist back to nearly a twenty-degree angle.

"I didn't think my arm would ever be right again," he breathed.

"Why not?" Edie asked, biting back a smile.

He had a constellation of dark freckles across one cheek, which he scratched as if they were bug bites. "I guess 'cause it made such a...*cr-r-runch* when I came down on it. Like a stick breaking. My arm just bent back, way back, like it could never straighten out again."

Edie managed to conceal her wince of pain, knowing it was part of the healing process, this needing to relate the gory details of a frightening episode to another person in a post-traumatic-stress way of reliving it in order to be purged of it.

Which, once begun, now seemed to pour out of Sam. "I got up, and my hand flopped down a little in this really weird way. That's when Mrs. Baxter came around the side of the staircase. She turned white as a sheet when she saw my hand. I thought, uh-oh, and I started to get scared. I tried to move my fingers but it hurt too much."

She forestalled any further confession from Sam by asking, "Who's Mrs. Baxter?"

"She's my sitter. Kind of an older lady—"

"Whose heart probably isn't used to seeing such daring." She set her hand on the boy's knee to emphasize her point, and for the first time Sam permitted the caress. "You must take more care, Sam. The next time you think about trying something kind of chancy like that, would you run it by your dad or Mrs. Baxter first? Would you do that, for me? It'd ease my mind so much."

Dark lashes fell, then lifted again to reveal his clear-eyed gaze. "Okay. I don't want people to worry 'bout me."

"I know you don't, Sam." She thought of the boy's father, remembering the look of stark fear that had come over his features when made to picture Sam's accident—along with the anger in his eyes when he reprimanded her for putting more ideas into the boy's head.

Perhaps Holden had been right in that judgment. The last thing she wanted was for Sam to hurt himself again. Well, maybe her words to him now would help make up for that.

"You know, it might be best to stick to regular sports for a while," she said. "Are there any you like you look forward to getting back to?"

One cheek dented as he thought. "No. I used ta play soccer back in Chicago. And Little League. And I took swim lessons at the Y, and I was a junior member of the Museum of Natural History. Uh—only that's not a sport."

Edie gave him a bright yellow weight and showed him how to hold it while curling his wrist forward. "You don't participate in any stuff like that here?"

"Well, Mrs. Baxter doesn't drive too well. She says there're nuts out there on the road and it's enough for her to make it over to our house every afternoon without havin' to go out again."

"Sounds like my aunt," Edie said on a chuckle. "Who took you around to your activities in Chicago?"

She knew the moment she'd asked the question what the answer was, especially when Sam's rhythm faltered ever so slightly.

"Keep going, Sam, I'm doing the counting. Seven more reps," she interjected, sparing him from an answer. "I'm guessing you probably get plenty of playing in, anyway, with your friends."

"I don't have any friends," Sam said.

Edie, who'd been reaching for an elastic therapy band on the shelf under the plinth, was brought up short. She shot Sam a glance. "Not from around your neighborhood?"

He shook his head. "Dad and me live in a town house where there aren't any kids my age. A singles complex, Mrs. Baxter calls it." His tongue snaked out to hook over his upper lip in a way Edie found especially endearing. "She doesn't like it. It's all people who drive red cars. And the girls wear skimpy swimsuits around the pool, so she doesn't like to take me down there anymore. Not a place for children, she tol' my dad."

From Sam's description, Edie had to agree with Mrs. Baxter. The situation sounded bewildering at best. "What about the kids in your class at school, Sam? Don't you play with them?"

He shrugged in answer, his attention now a little too fixed on what he was doing.

"Sam."

The boy glanced up.

"You could ask some of the boys over after school, couldn't you? Maybe one at a time, if Mrs. Baxter can't handle a bunch of you. You know, to have a game of catch or kick the soccer ball around."

"Where would me and a friend play if I had one?" His gaze fell. He seemed embarrassed to make such an admission. "We don't have a yard, just this little patio. My room isn't big enough to play anything fun. I don't think kids were meant to live there much."

That was why he'd invented his own entertainment, impractical as it had been, Edie thought. "So why *do* you live there?"

"I dunno." His forehead screwed up in both effort and thought. "I guess 'cause the furniture came with it. Dad didn't bring any of our old stuff, 'cept for clothes and a couple of other things. He said it was just temp'rary and we'd buy new furniture once we got settled. But Dad's been real busy since we got here," the boy hastily explained.

"I'm sure he has been." Edie knew she was asking a lot of questions but couldn't seem to stop. A very disturbing picture was forming in her head, which was beginning to negate the favorable one she'd been fashioning of Holden McKee. She needed to take her own advice, though, and not jump into a situation without thoroughly evaluating it. Not jump to conclusions about certain doctors who put their work—or their problems—first, to the exclusion of other considerations, most important the welfare of their families.

"Just how long have you lived at this complex, Sam?"

Another shrug, this one a bit reluctant. "We moved a couple of weeks after school started here."

That probably meant September, Edie calculated. And here it was early May. Nine months of living essentially in a friendless limbo with little means to set down roots.

And with nary a familiar belonging, not to mention a father who'd been essentially unavailable, to ease him through the transition of learning to live without his mother...

To her utter dismay, quick tears sprang to Edie's eyes, and she turned away under pretense of looking for her pen rather than have Sam notice. Her back to him, she struggled for control, but the thought of this little boy enduring such a tragedy alone struck her soul-deeply.

Of a sudden, that image of the boy in the woods flooded her vision, his face filled with an anguish so acute as to be overwhelming.

"Were you...were you allowed to keep anything of your mother's to remember her by, Sam?" It was the toughest question of all, but she had to ask it. She had to know.

He made no answer, and Edie turned back to him. He'd stopped doing the wrist curls, the back of his hand resting on his knee, his head down. "I-I had a bear she made me when I was little, but when I got here I put it in the giveaway box. I'm too big for that kind of stuff now."

Fresh tears filled her eyes. "That's all?"

His chin sank another inch closer to his chest, chestnut hair hanging down. "Dad gave me a picture of...of her to put in my room. But I stuck it away in my dresser."

She couldn't see his face at all. His voice, though, was expressionless. "Why, Sam?" she whispered.

"It...hurt. It hurt Dad."

He started up the curls with renewed vigor, setting his attention to the task with the same focus she imagined his father gave to anything he did.

Through a blur, she took in the set of Sam's shoulders—held so like Holden's, sturdy and strong. But there was a drip of what looked like dried ketchup down the front of his T-shirt, reminding her that he was just a little boy, and one who shouldn't have to take on the worries of the world at his age.

Edie stayed him with a light hand over his. "That should be enough reps, champ," she said gently, her voice not quite steady. "You did great."

He looked up then, gaze homing in on her face, and this time Edie made no move to hide the tears in her eyes. She had promised herself not to turn away, and she wouldn't. Would not hold back her emotions—as if she could.

Yet she wondered if she was right to let him see how greatly his troubles affected her when Sam, his jaw set defiantly, said, "Y'know, I hate Texas! I wish we never came here. I wish...I wish..."

His gaze dropped yet again, and Edie knew without actually seeing them that now he fought back tears. She ached for the boy's loss and loneliness and regretted she'd ever brought the subject up.

"Oh, Sam," she murmured, wrapping her arms around him, not knowing what else to do. But he resisted, pushing her away automatically with his injured arm. Pain shot across his features.

She stepped back, giving him the space he seemed to need right now, though it went against her every instinct.

"Can I put my splint back on?" he mumbled. "I don't feel like any more therapy today."

Edie stifled a troubled sigh. "Of course, Sam. You've made really terrific progress. It won't hurt to quit a little early today." She thought about mentioning the exercises he should continue doing at home with his father's help, considered broaching the subject of forgoing the splint more often, but decided it might be best to go over both issues—along with a few others—alone with Holden.

As she helped Sam on with his splint, Edie wondered where she would find the perspective this time that would allow her to appeal to both Holden McKee's emotional and logical sides.

For she knew she must find her own balance in this matter, which was becoming more and more one of the heart—and soul.

Edie pulled into the parking lot at Grace Hospital, where Dr. McKee worked. She'd been unable to talk to Holden the previous afternoon, which was just as well. By making an appointment with him today, she'd had some time to think and had arranged her argument in a clear, coherent order. She sincerely hoped it would impress her point upon Holden without getting him up in arms against her. His cynicism had a formidable bite to it, but she felt she was up to any debate.

So why was her heart thumping away like the bass drum at a rock concert?

She entered the hospital through Emergency Admittances and made her way through a scarcely populated waiting room to the desk. She'd found it interesting to discover his specialty was in emergency care. Given that fact, it made more sense that he didn't ascribe to her definition of health care, that of helping patients to manage their emotional states as part of helping them to come to terms with their physical crises. ER doctors dealt with the here and now of medical treatment. Rare was the instance they continued a doctor-patient relationship once the patient was released or consigned to the care of a specialist or their regular physician.

Which made it easy to remain uninvolved, distant, detached.

Well, and no surprise there. Somehow she'd had a feeling his specialty wasn't pediatrics.

Edie had opened her mouth to ask for Dr. McKee when she spotted him coming out of an examining room. At the same time, he lifted his gaze from the chart in his hands and spied her in what seemed to Edie to be an almost fateful meeting of glances. Obviously he'd been pulled out of a moment of concentration; still, he didn't look entirely displeased to see her.

Her heart stepped up its beat as he strode toward her.

He wore a set of surgical scrubs, the drawstring pants tied snug around a trim waist, the V-neck of the top showing a triangle of dark hair, the shortened sleeves revealing muscular forearms.

"Be with you in a sec, Ms. Turner," he said, leaning against the desk and scribbling instructions on the chart. She'd noticed before how he had strong, capable hands. Abruptly, the moment when she'd marked that feature came tumbling back to her as she remembered his fingers in her hair, stroking a lock of it with complete absorption, as if he couldn't tear his eyes away.

Neither could she now as she became fascinated with how the scrubs' faded color brought out the sea-green highlights in his eyes as he looked at her—with one dark eyebrow raised.

"Ms. Turner?" he said, snapping her out of her daze. "You wanted to see me?"

"Uh, yes." She felt her face warm up, her gaze falling of its own will to his wide chest.

He seemed to take her inspection as a question. "I don't normally wear scrubs on my shift, but I had a six-month-old this morning with projectile vomiting, which doesn't leave you with much option but to change."

He actually smiled then, and Edie saw for the first time what a handsome man he really was, with an angular jaw and a well-shaped nose. And those eyes, which drew her in instantly.

She wondered how she'd keep her focus on Sam during the coming conversation. Holden's presence was commanding at the very least, and here in his element, where he felt the most control, it was staggering.

"Is there somewhere we can have a seat to talk?" she

asked, wanting to get this over with, with her equilibrium intact.

Holden glanced around. "Sure. There's a courtyard just outside. Let me just grab a soda."

He led the way to a charming spot between two wings of the hospital, with a fountain situated among a stand of live oaks and landscaped flower beds. They had it to themselves, fortunately.

Or unfortunately, depending how one chose to look at it, Edie thought as she crossed to a stone bench and sat, the doctor dropping down beside her. She'd worn her hair tied back rather than loose today, and realized only now why she'd done so.

She clasped her hands in her lap and decided to plunge right in.

"Dr. McKee, have you ever thought of buying a house in this area?"

Holden looked at her in surprise. "I was under the impression you wanted to talk about Sam. He seemed upset last night when we got home."

"This *is* about Sam. You see, he told me a little about where you live, and I have to say, Doctor, it doesn't sound very child-friendly. He said he has no place to play with any other kids he might ask over."

Warming to her subject, she turned to face him straight on. "Not that he would, which is another matter. Sam feels he has no friends, and where would he have the opportunity to make any?"

"Why, at school, of course," Holden said, frowning.

"But you know how children build social skills. It can't be done only at school. They need to form friendships that aren't limited by that environment." She hesitated, biting her lip. "Sam said he'd taken part in a lot of activities in Chicago. But he hasn't gotten into any here for some reason."

As she'd anticipated, that brought out even a greater frown, complete with lowered eyebrows, as if she were a disobedient child. "Obviously, the situation's different here than in Chicago. It would be great if I worked at a job with regular hours but I don't, and I'm not going to apologize for that."

He took an impatient swig of his Coke. "Sam has only to ask and he can have friends over to play, or go over to their houses. He knows that. If he was interested in an activity of some kind, believe me, I'd do everything in my power to make arrangements with other parents to get him to and from it."

Did he actually hear himself? "Really, Dr. McKee. Do you honestly see a six-year-old taking such initiative in a new and still unfamiliar place, one he's had no reason to want to become a part of?"

The muscle in Holden's jaw bulged. "He'll adjust, Ms. Turner. It just takes time."

"*How* much time? Sam hates it here, and can you blame him? He's had no way to set down roots."

Edie stood and paced a few restless yards away, then pivoted to face Holden, hands clasped behind her back. "You know, there are properties that come up for sale every once in a while out in Parker, where I live with my aunt. Some have wooded acreages attached to them just right for exploring or building a clubhouse. A lot of places even have stables." An idea popped into her head. "There're riding clubs that give lessons, too, where Sam could get into a *real* Texas sport, horseback riding. Maybe even enter some competitions for his age group."

Holden drained his pop can and set it aside before standing as well. "Yes, and I can see it now—one hundred and one more ways for my son to break every bone in his body."

"Oh, good grief." Edie set her fists on her hips. "You act as if he'd be completely unsupervised or without rules. You're not setting him loose in the woods to fend for himself against the elements."

Gray-green sparks shot from his eyes. *Good*, she thought.

Maybe she'd make a permanent dent in that impassive exterior of his.

Figuring herself in for a pound, Edie went on. "And what if he did? Sam needs some place he can just be a boy. So he gets a scrape and needs a tetanus shot, or he learns the hard way how to steer a wide path around a hill of fire ants or a patch of poison ivy!"

"What about getting bit by a rabid skunk or falling down a ravine or God knows what else!"

"Well, if it's not those things, Dr. McKee, it'll be something else. You've already had one experience dealing with Sam's curiosity venturing out with his attempt to fly!"

"I believe I've heard enough, Ms. Turner," Holden said from between clenched teeth. "I can see now why Sam was so upset—"

"What about *you*, Dr. McKee?" Edie interrupted with a persistence that seemed almost foolhardy, even to herself. She was losing sight of her purpose here, losing control of herself. "You work in a sterile environment all day long, with this courtyard probably the only bit of nature you come into contact with."

She took two steps toward him, hands spread before her. "Wouldn't it be nice not to live in such an antiseptic atmosphere? If you lived in the country, you'd discover it can be wonderful to unwind in a place away from the city, in your own retreat or refuge. Maybe it'd loosen you up a little, too!"

He stalked forward, grim and intent. "You seem determined to step way beyond your purview, don't you, Ms. Turner?"

"And you seem determined to keep your son from putting his mother's death behind him and getting on with living!"

"I am not!" he nearly shouted.

"What do you call it, then? You've completely sacrificed every bit of your old life, moved away from or done away with any reminders of her, yet you've done nothing to fill the void! You can't keep Sam—or yourself—cooped up in a box, you know. You can't keep life from happening to either of you. No one can live that way. And living is what you've been left here to do."

Yes, she felt desperate—desperate to make him understand. She'd known she cared about Sam, but she hadn't known till now how much, for if it hadn't been for that little boy, she'd have nothing to do with his pigheaded father!

She tried again. "I know it's hard to move on, Doctor—"

"Do you?" He stood toe to toe with her now, almost looming over her, his face vivid with emotion. "How could you possibly presume to *begin* to understand what I'm going through?"

Edie didn't shrink from him, didn't let herself falter as she gazed up at him. "Because barely a year ago I lost both my parents, my mother to a degenerative disease she'd battled for five years. And all that time, the hope and promise of recovery got yanked from her—from us all—again and again. After she died, Dad simply…pined away for her, almost like he felt there was nothing left to live for." Her voice cracked. "I guess there wasn't. Two months later, I had to let him go, too."

His gaze darkened, and she saw that at last she'd touched him as understanding, compassion—and something like reluctant recognition—flared in the back of his eyes.

"Is that why you chose to go into physical therapy?" he asked.

She nodded. "Yes, to care for my mother. But also because I wanted to care for other people, too. I needed to…to—"

Oh, how to explain it? Yes, it was a hard thing to face, being left behind. There were no words to convey that feeling of lonely emptiness inside.

But still, she had never lost hope, never stopped believing in the promise of the future. And for whatever reason, she found she needed to gift others with that solace. Needed the connection best found in a simple touch, that sign that said *we have each other*.

Edie wanted so to reach out to Holden right now and share that uncomplicated message. Yet to her utter confusion, it was he who reached out to her, although not in the form of a touch.

"I'm...sorry," he murmured. His gray-green gaze became deeper still. "Sorry for your loss. You do know."

She shook her head as she sought complete truth with him. "The death of an elderly parent isn't the same as losing your beloved in an untimely manner. So no, I don't know, but I *can* imagine how making sense of that kind of injustice must be brutal on the human spirit."

Her chin dropping, she could say no more, memories and doubts crowding in on her and attacking her own resolve to move on, to stay in touch with life and feel it coursing through her, filling her own empty places from within. But it was so hard! And still sometimes, she felt so empty.

Edie swallowed urgently, her eyes filling with tears.

Then Holden spoke.

"I *have* lived in the country, you know—rural East Texas, to tell the truth," he said, his breath stirring her hair.

Her head came up in surprise at the hushed tone in his voice. Almost reverent.

"The piney woods are beautiful there," he continued musingly. "The needles make this cushiony carpet you can walk on even in bare feet, your every step muffled. The smell of pine surrounds you, like a cloud. When the sun shines down through the branches, it looks just like something out of a painting...."

Closing her eyes, Edie could picture it exactly. "Is that why you moved back to Texas? To show Sam where you lived when you were his age? Or maybe for him to be near family?" she asked, thrilled that he was sharing his thoughts with her.

When he didn't answer, Edie opened her eyes to find Holden scrutinizing her upturned face. His gaze dove deeply into hers, just as he had that first time, intimately, searchingly. Like he would look at a lover.

His gaze fell to her lips.

Would he kiss her? she wondered on a precipice of anticipation. Did she want him to?

His arm lifted, and her breath stopped in her chest as his fingers grazed along her jawline to push an escaped tendril of her hair back, then curve down around behind her ear.

It was barely a touch at all—and not quite a caress. Still, it affected Edie as deeply as if Holden *had* kissed her. And she realized that words were not enough, that this kind of touching was what made life and living real.

Was this what had been missing from her life? she asked herself. She didn't know, but it had her yearning for more. So much more.

She saw a yearning in Holden's eyes, too, as she'd seen it before. Although now it seemed his was nostalgic, a looking back, while her longing was for what might be.

For as she looked into his eyes, she knew it was not her face Holden saw as he gazed at her so intently, but someone else's.

It didn't take much pondering to guess who that might be. His dead wife.

Edie realized only then how she wanted with all her being a love such as that—one that seemed greater than this world, the power and depth and realness of it outlasting this mortal life, as her parents had had. As Holden had apparently had with his Sam's mother.

A fist closed around her heart, making her want to protect herself. She stepped back, out of his reach and away from his touch.

For a moment he stood with his arm still outstretched, almost as if he were a statue. Then, with a muttered oath, Holden turned away, picking up his empty pop can and considering it with undue attention.

"No," he said, as if there'd been no break in the conversation. "I have no desire ever to go back to East Texas. What for? There's no one and nothing there for me."

Edie frowned, that same protectiveness making her oddly defensive. "No? Well, then, don't you think you owe it to Sam to put down roots *here* and let him get on with life?"

"Yes, I do have Sam to think of." He gave a short nod that grated on Edie in its dismissal of her concerns. "No one could accuse you of not caring for your patients' welfare, could they, Ms. Turner?"

Fed up, Edie retorted, "Is that something a person might accuse you of, Dr. McKee?"

He threw her a look over his shoulder, one eyebrow raised in that way he had of saying everything by saying nothing. He seemed back in perfect control.

It annoyed her no end.

Holden's beeper went off. He checked the number on it. "I've got to get back."

Without a backward glance or goodbye, he started toward the door—away from her.

She wasn't going to let him get away scot-free.

"Fine. Go bury yourself in your work," Edie called after him. "But the fact remains, Dr. McKee—you have one very lonely, unhappy son. What are you going to do about that?"

He turned, hands hanging on the stethoscope around his neck. "Why do you care so much, Edie?"

She came up short. She knew why, but how to say it? How to convey it to this man who thought anyone who trusted in the future foolish, to say the least?

"I think...no, I believe it's because I feel I've been given a unique chance here to do something to really help another, and I've promised myself not to turn away."

I can't turn away, Edie thought but didn't say—despite her need to protect herself.

Holden chewed on the inside of his cheek as he regarded her. "I guess all I can say to that is, you want to go on a mission to rescue the world that's your problem. As for me I make no promises unless I know I can keep them.''

He strode off, a man who lived in the moment, as he eminently preferred to be, with a specific, tangible job to fulfill, which would be either solved or passed on to another to solve by the end of the day.

Yes, she understood that it was easier, more manageable for Holden this way—not to go out on a limb emotionally. But it couldn't go on forever, for either him or Sam. Something would happen, something else besides the terrible event that had already torn their lives in two.

What would be the key to save both these two souls from their isolation and loneliness? And the bigger question was: did it indeed rest with her?

Chapter Four

Holden pulled the door closed behind him and gave the fortyish man lying in the bed a quick glance as he continued to go over the test results in his hands.

"Hello again, Mr. Osgood," Holden said, coming to a stop at the bedside. The patient's color had improved and he seemed less anxious after the mild sedative he'd been given, but he was obviously more worried than in pain.

"Is it my heart, Doctor?" Osgood asked. "Did I have a heart attack? My dad died of one when he was only a few years older than I am right now."

"Yes, we've got that in your history—"

"I've got a wife and three kids at home, Doctor." He ran a hand across his forehead, paling again. "How are they gonna make it without me?"

"Well, with any luck, Mr. Osgood, they won't have to worry about that prospect for some time." Holden flashed him a brief smile, meant to reassure. "That's the good news. The electrocardiogram shows no irregularities and your blood work looks good. If you were having a heart attack, it would have shown up there. We've done another set of exams to determine whether your pain is cardiac-related, and that's more good news. It isn't, although Nurse Andersen here says you're still feeling that heartburn kind of feeling that brought you in here in the first place."

"Yeah, right here." The man pressed a fist to his chest above the breastbone.

Holden gave a confirming nod. "Well, given how the EKG came out, the more severe chest pains you had earlier were likely the result of stomach acidity and what we call esophageal reflux. It can give you the sort of pain in the heart region that you felt, when actually it's your stomach acting up. Do you have indigestion on a regular basis, Mr. Osgood?"

"Sure, but...but what's the bad news, Doctor?"

Holden clasped the clipboard in front of him. "There is no real bad news, unless you call advice to take it easier from now on—not work so hard, and engage in more leisure activities to help reduce your stress and worry—bad news."

The other man looked at Holden as if he were crazy. "But, Doctor, I can't slack off at work now! You heard what I said— my own father keeled over at forty-four, no warning, no nothing. What if that happens to me?"

"Certainly, I'm recommending your doctor schedule you for a treadmill heart scan and complete cardiovascular workup as soon as possible. As for your father's death, you have the advantage of much better diagnostic tests these days. With care, any potential problem could be mitigated by—"

"You don't understand!" Osgood dragged on the neck of his hospital gown as if it choked him. "We don't have near enough savings. My wife would have to go back to work. My littlest is only six months old!"

Holden fixed his patient with a piercing glare. "Fine, Mr. Osgood. Let's play that scenario out, since you're determined to do so. Say I told you with one-hundred percent certainty that you would die in three years. What would you do with that time?"

Taken aback, Osgood stuttered, "I-I...I don't know."

"Work like a madman? Divorce yourself from your family so you can devote every waking second to ensuring they're provided for?"

Holden found himself going on ruthlessly. "Forget about spending precious time with your wife and children, you've got to focus on getting all your affairs strictly in order, try to control every little bit of your world because you know, deep down, that any control you have is pure illusion. How could it be anything else? You're going to die! And you'd be one of the lucky ones—at least you'd know when and how it's going to happen. The problem is, even then it's not something you can *plan* for!"

Both Osgood and Nurse Andersen gaped at him.

Biting back the rest of his lecture, Holden scribbled his name at the bottom of the chart and shoved it at the nurse. "You're free to go, Mr. Osgood. Follow up with your regular doctor as soon as you can find the time."

He was out of the examining room and had gotten to the end of the corridor before he realized where he was going.

With a shove on the door, Holden nearly stumbled into the courtyard, startling a mockingbird who'd been pecking at a juniper berry on the ground. The bird took off in a flurry of white epaulets and a flick of his long tail before settling in the nearby live oak, where he cast a reproachful brown eye on the intruder.

Holden stared back. He'd seen that look before, and within the past few days—days in which that look, those words and a certain presence had slowly but surely found their way into his thoughts, disrupting his sleep and now his waking hours.

No doubt about it, Edie Turner was getting to him.

Cursing soundly, Holden broke a twig off the tree and almost stripped it of its foliage, but something made him instead brush his fingers over the glossy, dark-green leaves. The live oak spoke of Texas more than any other tree—except, perhaps, for the magnolia. He didn't care for either species much, would always consider the southern pine, with its long, limber needles and turpentine-scented sap, the tree most meaningful to any feelings he might have about his home state.

Which were?

Certainly, here was where he'd last felt at home.

Edie thought he should buy a house and put down roots, did she? Actually, Holden could see the logic in that suggestion. If he and Sam were ever to make a go of a life here, buying their own home would help. Sam was the one who'd really benefit—*he* was the sapling, with the greatest chance of a transplant taking hold, of the land getting into his roots and providing him with a sense of belonging.

Was that why he had taken a position here? Holden wondered.

Meditatively, he sat on the stone bench, resting his elbows on his knees as he bent over in thought, his fingers still caressing the oak leaves. He could come up with no better answer to his question than that he'd felt drawn here. At the time, he'd thought it was the opportunity to work in a private hospital, where the emergencies tended to be less intense, less...intrusive. Yet Holden wondered now if his motivation for returning to Texas had sprung from some other source within him—

He sat up straight. Good grief, now not just Edie Turner but also her touchy-feely "picking up on things" way of thinking was getting to him! It was all too close, these undefined feelings about her and what she seemed able to rouse in him: deep, dark yearnings for something he had long ago given up holding out hope of having. And yet how she called up in him an unholy dread of reaching too far....

Holden stood, restless to move but without direction. At other times he wanted to shake her, make her understand that it wasn't so simple a matter as she made it out to be: Buy a house with a yard, and Sam'll put down roots. Take the boy on a sentimental journey to East Texas, and guaranteed they'd find instant resolution to any grief both of them might have. Just state it to the world that you're going to accept what's happened to you and that you're moving on and presto! You do it.

The hell of it was, Holden wanted all those things for Sam, so much: the trust that came from believing in the constancy of today, the peace derived from reconciling with the past, the hope for tomorrow born from taking life on faith. Yes, he wanted all that for Sam.

But as for himself, Holden believed it was too late.

Bleakly, he let his gaze roam the manicured courtyard. To be sure, it was a touch of nature, as Edie had said, but it wasn't his style. Too groomed. The flowers were pretty, though, especially the roses.

Rose. His wife, and the mother of his child. Thinking of her always brought a distinctive kind of pain to his own chest, calling up old fears the same way Osgood's pain had brought on the fear what would happen to his father would happen to him. In that way, Holden and Osgood were like peas in a pod: afraid of failing to be there for their loved ones when they needed him most.

Yet for Holden the pain went even deeper, for he also felt guilty of not loving others enough. Otherwise, why would they be yanked from him without warning, without reason, again and again?

But then no one, not even Edie Turner, with all her talk of reaching out to love again, could make any guarantees. Perhaps he had no control over what happened, hard as that was for him to deal with, but neither did she.

No, he couldn't let Sam get too fond of Edie. He simply wouldn't stand for Sam having his heart torn from him when things didn't turn out as he'd been led to believe.

Oh, he could hear Edie's argument to that: *But you've still got to try to find purpose wherever you are, whatever's happened, to try to put down roots and go on with your life.* He'd seen it in her eyes: that was what she was trying to do on her own. She believed in the promise of the future. She had hope, not to mention the tenacity of a bulldog and the fervency of a revival preacher. And the passion of a woman who would settle for nothing but the best for herself and those she cared about. Would settle for nothing but their best from them, for she gave her all in return. Always.

Holden tossed away the twig, which startled the mockingbird into flight again. He turned his eyes upward to watch it go and continued staring up at the blue sky between the concrete gray buildings—and knew something of Sam's desire to fly. But if that little scene just now with Mr. Osgood had proved anything to Holden, it was that there were just so many more places left in his own heart where he could escape to.

For his greatest fear was not that he would reach too far, but not far enough. Again.

Edie grinned across the car seat at the sight of Sam, who had his nose practically glued to the passenger window as he watched two colts gamboling in a fenced pasture along FM544 heading out of Dallas toward the rural township of Parker.

She'd known he would be enthralled. What kid wouldn't? It was one of the best aspects about Dallas, being surrounded by lakes and farms and ranches. Where else could you see longhorns grazing along a fence line within a few feet of four-lane traffic!

Of course, Sam's father wasn't too thrilled with her right now. In fact, she had the impression Holden was pretty peeved with her for seeming to engineer this impromptu outing for Sam. But when he'd dropped the boy off for his PT, Holden *had* hurriedly instructed her to work out Sam's getting home with Mrs. Baxter, since he had to get back to the hospital and wouldn't be able to break away till after the clinic's closing time. Edie had had no problem convincing Sam's sitter over the phone that Dr. McKee wouldn't at all mind having to retrieve his son from way over in Parker. That way the older woman wouldn't have to venture out in Dallas rush-hour traffic, and she could get on home to her supper and *Wheel of Fortune* right on time.

Edie had waited until she knew Mrs. Baxter was on the road before paging Holden to inform him of the plan. Naturally, if he'd objected, she would have driven Sam home and stayed with him until his father got there, but he didn't. Although his voice could at best have been described as terse as he asked for directions to her house, he said he trusted he would not get there and find Sam wrapped in a sheet and suspended upside down from a tree branch like a cocoon.

Her chest had expanded with pleasure. Holden wouldn't have even come close to joking about such a thing if he didn't believe Sam was safe with her.

Little steps, it seemed, were the best way to manage both McKee men.

"Does your aunt have horses, too?" Sam asked, practically wriggling in his seat.

"Yup, she's got a pretty sorrel mare she calls Fancy and a black gelding, name of Hercules," she told him, exaggerating her Texas drawl.

"Wow" was all Sam could say.

Edie pulled off the main road and drove up the long lane to her aunt's home, a modest plantation-style clapboard set among a stand of white-barked birches. She'd called to give Hazel some warning of whom she would be bringing home— Edie had already confided in her aunt some of the details about this special patient—and the older woman met them at the door. The cozy smell of baking wafted out from behind her.

"Welcome, welcome," she said cheerily, sticking out a gnarled hand to the boy. "I'm Aunt Hazel."

Sam took her hand without hesitation. "My name is Sam."

"And don't you look just like a Sam!" She bent at the waist and peered at him from behind her bifocals. "Do ya like chocolate chip cookies, Sam?"

"Yes, ma'am, very much," the boy answered politely as Edie and Hazel exchanged private smiles over his head.

"Well, we don't stand on ceremony 'round here. Grab yourself a chair and a glass of milk and dig in. I gotta have room on the rack for the next batch comin' out of the oven."

Twenty minutes later Hazel was lacking half a dozen cookies and Sam had a smile of satiation to go along with the smear of chocolate across one cheek. Unable to resist, Edie leaned over and rubbed it off with a napkin. Brow puckering, Sam gave the spot another swipe.

"After I change into some shorts, you want to go explore a little bit?" she suggested.

"Can we do it on horses?" he asked, eyes wide with an anticipation she had seen little of in him.

Which made it incredibly hard for Edie to disappoint him. Holden was right to put his trust in her, for she wouldn't endanger his son in any way. "I'm afraid not today. We can go pet them, but riding's out until we check with your dad. Maybe next time, okay?"

The expectation in his eyes dimmed but didn't extinguish itself completely. "Will there be a next time?"

"I—" Edie hesitated, recalling Holden's caution of not making promises one couldn't keep. She reached out to smooth down that spiky hair, but Sam ducked from under her hand. She let her arm drop to the table, still outstretched toward him. "I can't say for certain, but I'll do my best to make sure you get that chance."

Thankfully, the youngster seemed satisfied with her answer. Doing her best was all she had ever promised him. It was all anyone could expect of another.

The early evening sun was still warm upon their backs as

Sam and Edie made their way along. Their rustlings past sent creatures and birds scurrying deep into the brush on either side of the track, though here and there a fat squirrel or iridescent black grackle found the courage to stand up to them and give them a good scolding for disrupting their world.

Edie drew in a huge lungful of fresh air. How she loved it here! Holden wasn't the only one who needed to escape from the workaday atmosphere and find rejuvenation in a bit of nature.

The previous night's rain had revived the scents of loam and prairie grasses, sweet and fertile, and washed clean the land clear up to the treetops, making their glossy foliage look like it had been infused from within with an emerald glow as the breeze stirred their leaves. She'd grown up looking at a lot of horizon and missed that stark, wide-open-spaces side of Texas. But this side would do her fine, too.

Edie had let Sam lead the way, and she cherished the opportunity to observe him unnoticed. Her gaze roved over the cowlick in his shiny dark hair, to the stalwart set of his small shoulders and the jaunty, tripping-along way he walked, both arms outstretched like wings—even his healing one—to capture the sensation of the waist-high grass brushing against his skin.

It made his continued avoidance of her caresses that much more conspicuous, Edie thought. Her touch seemed to disturb him, and she'd guessed it was because he was holding so much inside him that any token of empathy from another might burst the dam and send too many emotions flooding unchecked to the surface.

It rent her heart. She'd truly have done or given anything to free him of his anguish.

A nicker in the distance had her squinting that direction.

"There they are," Edie said. "Fancy and Hercules, just down the hill under that pecan tree. Do you see them?"

Sam craned his neck, his perspective a few feet lower than

hers. "Yeah, I do!" He threw a roguish look over his shoulder at her. "Let's run!" he cried, and took off before she could reply.

Edie laughed, delighted. Yes, this outing was definitely good for him. Her heart lifted infinitesimally.

She followed him at an easy lope as he tore pell-mell down the incline, excitement in every step. He even gave a little leap, still trying, despite his accident, to experience what it would be like to fly, if only for a brief moment out of time.

He had fast become very dear to her, if possible even more than when he'd first captured her heart as he stood there with his injured arm pressed to his chest and that look of utter abandonment in his large gray eyes—

Terrified. Panting. Legs churning, churning for all they're worth, but it's not enough.

Edie tripped but kept going, even as the images flickered across her mind's eye like the dappling of sunlight and shadow under the trees.

"That's it. Keep going!" The boy held out his hand to her, unbearable fear in his gray-green eyes.

Her own eyes watered, blinding her even more. She threw out one arm, groping the air to find her way. Her breath came on a sob.

She struggled, yearning toward him. But it was hard. Too much.

"No! Don't do it! Don't you dare give—"

Edie went down with a crash, palms and knees grinding into the ground, the impact nearly enough to jar her teeth out of their sockets and certainly enough to shake loose the barrette securing her hair.

Too late, she remembered to roll with the fall, and she finally came to a stop flat on her back in the grass, shaken and battered and completely disoriented.

What in heaven's name had happened?

With trembling fingers she brushed her hair out of her eyes

and looked up with perfect clarity at a big white cloud in the sky, hardly believing that a moment ago she'd been unable to see three feet ahead of her.

It had been like living a nightmare in broad daylight, complete with larger-than-life panic and a feeling of entrapment and everything. Most of all it had been eerily real.

Groaning, Edie sat up. The heels of her hands were still numb from the force of her fall, although the nerve endings under the scraped skin on her knees were screaming with pain. She gingerly wiped pebbles and bits of twigs and earth off them with the tail of her T-shirt. The bleeding wasn't too bad, but she'd have a couple of doozies of bruises.

What did these...these images mean? Something that was going to happen? She'd never considered herself prescient. Why was Sam so afraid in them? Certainly, a murk of danger had loomed all around him—

Instantly, Edie was on her feet and sprinting down the track, her heart in her throat.

"Sam!" she screamed, nearly beyond panic. "Sam! Where are you? *Answer me!*"

She almost mowed him down as she came charging into the clearing, her whirlwind entrance sending both horses rearing back, heads raised high, the whites showing around their eyes.

"I'm sorry." Sam grabbed a handful of her T-shirt to keep from being bowled over. "I was just playin'—"

Her arms wrapped around the boy and crushed him to her.

"Oh, Sam," she wheezed from a throat constricted with emotion, her lungs near collapse. He was safe! For now.

"What happened?" Struggling, he pulled away from her, his gaze frantically searching hers. It lit on the blood dotting the front of her shirt. Sam blanched. "Edie, what's wrong!"

Heavens, she was frightening him. Gathering her wits, Edie gave a shaky laugh and showed him one of her hands. "Clumsy me, I fell down! Serves me right for not looking where I was stepping. Must have been a gopher hole."

"But why were you yelling my name, like you were scared?" His hands still clung to the tail of her shirt, as if he were afraid to let her go for fear she'd disappear before his eyes, so tenuous was his trust of the world.

"Because I *was* scared." Unable to stop herself, Edie drew the boy against her again, needing to feel his realness perhaps more than he did hers. She bit her lip, and decided a white lie was in order. "You don't know horses very well, and Fancy and Hercules don't know you at all. They might have shied and knocked you down. I didn't want you to try to approach them without some instruction and a piece of carrot."

"Oh." The word was muffled against her. "I thought maybe...I dunno. You were just so scared."

"I know. But I'm okay now."

And you're okay. Edie closed her eyes as she stroked her fingers through his hair, over and over. She could have stayed like this forever, holding him close. Holding him safe.

But Sam evidently felt differently. With a reluctance that seemed more for her benefit than his own, he tugged away and stood apart from her.

Head down, he scratched his nose. "So everything's all right?"

"Y-yes." It wasn't another fib, she told herself staunchly.

"Then can I pet the horses?"

She tried not to be disappointed or hurt. But her arms felt suddenly very empty. "Sure, Sam."

For his sake, Edie tried to act normally as she pulled a piece of carrot from her pocket with her battered hand and showed him how to balance it on his palm to let the horses come to him.

Within minutes, Hercules had ambled over, large ebony head bobbing, and gently nuzzled the carrot from Sam's open hand.

Sam looked up at her, a little scared of the animal's size

but also clearly tickled, and Edie found she could smile back at him, albeit somewhat unsteadily.

Because an idea came to her that gave her a sudden surge of hope, even as that vision of impending danger stayed with her, along with her growing fear of not knowing where or when it would strike again.

Or how to fight it.

By the time they trekked back to the house, the sun had dropped behind the trees, though it still backlit their branches, like silhouettes cut from black paper. Edie was glad to see the glow shining forth from Hazel's kitchen windows, a beacon in the gathering dusk. Hazel herself was taking advantage of the cooling evening air to chat over the fence with her neighbor, Olive, who was of an age and attitude with Hazel, which was to say seventy and fiercely independent. Edie still found ways to help Olive out and keep an eye on her, since the older woman was diabetic and had no kin in the immediate area.

"Sakes alive, Edie," Hazel exclaimed when she saw the patches of dirt and blood on her niece's knees. "What happened to you?"

"I tripped and fell," Edie explained on a laugh, hoping it didn't sound forced. "I guess I wasn't paying attention."

She should have known, though, that her excuse would earn her a skeptical look from Hazel. There were two things Edie was not, and that was either clumsy or inattentive.

Leaving Sam with the two older women, she excused herself to go clean up and put antibiotic ointment on her various scrapes.

Edie returned to find her aunt and Olive engaged in their daily comparison of their aches and pains.

"How *is* your leg today, Olive?" Edie asked.

Grasping the ball atop the pole to the chain link fence, Olive raised the orthopedic-shod toe of the mentioned limb, encased in support hose, like a ballerina at the bar. "Better, though the doctor says I need to keep my circulation up or I might be in for some real trouble with it. I've been trying to get around a little bit on it, but it sure enough is like walking on an achy old stump."

Edie drew Sam into the conversation with a change of subject. "Did Sam tell you he's one of my PT patients? And doing wonderfully, too. His arm is coming along very well."

"Your arm, did she say?" Olive squinted. Sam dutifully held the limb up for closer inspection. "What'd you do to it?"

"I was trying to fly like David Copperfield and came down on it wrong," he said with his old reluctance, Edie noticed.

If he expected a lecture on letting his imagination get the better of him from either of these two ladies, he was going to be disappointed.

"Tried to fly!" Olive's penciled eyebrows escalated on her forehead. "Well, you're a braver soul than I am, Sam. Me, I like to keep in constant contact with ol' terra firma."

Hazel agreed with a theatrical shudder. "Any flyin' needs done, I can do it just fine a-horseback."

Sam's eyes rounded. "Does it really feel like flying?"

Hazel looked at him thoughtfully. "Well, now that I think about it, I'd have to say it comes pretty darn close. You liked my two babies, then?"

"Edie would only let me pet their noses, but next time I want to do more."

Edie could see the prospect of getting up on a horse become even more set in the boy's mind, which definitely would not make Holden happy. She wondered if she should have brought Sam out to Hazel's then remembered her inspiration of a few minutes ago.

"Is Jazzy around?" she asked Olive.

"She should be, somewhere." Olive gave an ear-splitting whistle. "Jazzy! Here, girl!"

The black lab had evidently not been far, just indiscernible from the burgeoning twilight, as she came trotting over.

Edie peered over the fence. "The pups aren't all gone, are they? I thought Sam would like to see them."

"Nope. I only got one left, though. They go fast with as good a pedigree as Jazzy here has." Olive reached down and gave the dog a pat on the head. "I don't breed her but once every two years. A girl deserves a break, after all. Don'tcha, Jazz?"

The labrador panted her agreement. A smaller, snub-nosed version of the dog insinuated itself between her front legs and gave a ferocious bark, in falsetto, at the strangers on the other side of the fence.

"That's my little watchdog," Olive said, chuckling.

Sam stepped forward, hooking his fingers through the chain link and asking, as Edie had hoped he would, "Oh, can I hold it?"

"Sure. Lemme just—" Olive bent down with a huff of effort and caught the puppy under its belly "—get ahold of the little rascal."

Over the fence the fat puppy came with whimpers of indignation at being snatched from safety and passed around like a sack of potatoes. Hazel reached out to lend a hand of support before Sam caught the squirming body against him.

If Edie had been worried at all that Sam wouldn't respond to the irresistible attraction of a puppy, her concerns were put firmly to rest as the youngster cradled the creature in his arms and stroked a hand over the nappy baby fur, knowing with some little-boy instinct how to calm the pup.

The whimpers died as the puppy found Sam's hand and sniffed it. A pink tongue sneaked out to taste his skin.

With that contact, boy and dog bonded with the completeness of blood relatives. Edie watched as he cuddled the little body to him with none of the hesitation or reserve he displayed with her, holding on to the puppy as if he would never let it go.

An odd pang, a mixture of hurt and regret, stabbed her in

the midsection. She had hoped he would respond this way to the puppy, and yet...

Sam looked up, eyes shining almost incandescently. It was as if he were a whole different child than from a moment ago—a whole different child than Edie had ever seen before.

Alarms clanged a warning in her head that she had made a huge mistake in judgment, just as Sam confirmed it by asking, his voice alive with hope, "Can I have him?"

Her heart sank. Oh, why hadn't she seen this coming!

She bent down to him, putting herself at his eye level. "Sam...sweetheart—that's not what I was thinking when I asked about your seeing the puppy."

"Actually, I was kinda holdin' this young'un back to keep," Olive jumped in, obviously understanding Edie's predicament. "There's just somethin' sorta special about this little one—"

"I'd treat him special!" Sam interrupted. "I'd take really, really, really good care of him!" He tightened his clasp on the puppy. "Wouldn't I, Edie?"

"I've no doubt you would, champ," Edie said gently, "but the puppy isn't up for adoption. Olive is keeping it for her own."

Pleading gray eyes turned up at the other woman. "But you already have a dog. I don't have anything."

Olive, bless her motherly heart, couldn't hold out against such an appeal. She opted to turn it over to the ultimate authority in every child's life. "You'll have to ask your parents."

The conditional part of Olive's statement went right over his head as Sam homed in on what he wanted to hear: the puppy could be his.

"I'll call him Hercules," he breathed, fingers stroking the velvet ears.

"Him?" Squinting one eye, Hazel gave the pup an expert

scrutiny. "I think you better come up with something a little less manly, Sam. This here's a female pup."

"Oh." The boy pondered other possibilities as over his head Edie had a silent but strident argument with her aunt not to encourage him.

But Hazel was as softhearted as Olive. "My advice is make it something you won't mind having to lean out your back door of an evening and shout out for the whole world to hear," she said. "How about...Beauty, as in Black Beauty?"

"Yeah. How about Beauty?" Without a single bit of concern for his healing arm, Sam held the pup up to his face and tried the name out. "Hi, Beauty!"

The round-as-a-sausage body wriggled in ecstasy. Her tongue flicked out in hopes of delivering more puppy kisses.

"She likes her name!" he exulted. And Sam laughed.

It was the first time Edie had heard such a sound from him. It came pealing from him again, like church bells ringing an angelus, as the puppy gave his face a thorough washing.

She had never heard such joy....

Then another sound, low and strangled, came from behind her. She turned. Holden stood there, the glow from the back porch light shining bright upon his face, limning each strong line in detail. He held himself very still, gaze intent as she had ever seen it, as if he sensed an enormous danger.

That's when Edie saw it: the face of the boy in her vision as he screamed a warning. But his eyes hadn't been pure gray like Sam's, she realized now. Instead, they were gray-green, like—

Recognition collided with her solar plexus. The boy was *Holden?*

But then, what about the danger she'd sensed? If not Sam, who was that for?

Chapter Five

Holden had not heard Sam's laughter in more than a year.

It rolled through him, reverberating in every crevice of his insides, like an earthquake traveling up through his feet, his legs, his torso, his arms and into his brain.

And shaking loose bits of mortar and brick in walls he'd thought built to last a lifetime.

He had *missed* it. Oh, how he had missed that sound, as one would a vital limb. Holden realized he had believed he'd never hear his son laugh again, so dire was his fear of daring to hope.

Sam caught sight of him and came running, his arms full of something. His face...unbelievably, his face radiated with joy, as if a miracle had occurred.

Maybe it had.

Holden dropped to one knee, arms outstretched.

Sam came to a screeching halt in front of his father. "Look, Dad! Look what I have!"

Holden's gaze fell to the bundle his son clutched to his chest. It was a black, brown-eyed puppy.

"Olive said I could keep her if I asked you first. Can I, Dad?" Sam begged. "Can I, please?"

The plea was one that had been heard by parents practically since the beginning of time, echoing up from the hearts of hundreds of thousands of children. Yet for Holden, it knocked loose another cache of buried memories to come thundering down on him in an avalanche. Open and exposed as he was at that moment, Holden felt trapped, duped. His only choice was to take steps to protect himself.

Dropping his arms, he slowly rose, willing himself to become detached and consider his son's request. It wasn't as if he hadn't known a time like this would come, sooner or later, this entreaty from Sam to make an animal, be it dog or cat, mouse or guinea pig, his own to love unconditionally. And who would love him back as completely and simply. Sam's counselor had even suggested a pet for the boy at one point, said it might help him heal if he had a purpose, something to teach him responsibility. More than that, though, a pet would take the focus off returning each day to a house without a mother waiting there and instead put it in the happy light of coming home to a little creature who'd greet him with licks and yips and uncontrollable tail-wagging.

Well, the counselor hadn't exactly put it that way. But that was how Holden had envisioned the scene, just as he'd pictured another, this one late at night, when the grief could be held at bay no longer, and having the solace of such an understanding little soul to wash the tears away—

Despite his resolve, childhood impressions of those first months after moving to Chicago bombarded him: the slow-moving air in that small, cramped room he shared with his cousin; the wail of sirens in the stillness of midnight, so starkly different from the sounds of crickets creaking and owls whoing; the lingering smells of cooking and disinfectant. Holden sometimes thought that, had he truly been left to himself within the familiar environment of his old life, he might have been able to face and eventually assuage his grief. There, he would have been unable to avoid his pain, and so might have gotten past it.

But now...oh, he'd been holding it back for so long, it seemed impossible to let go. Because the fact of the matter was, it hadn't had to be that way. If he hadn't been so foolhardy, so reckless, he wouldn't have had to have lain in that room with the lonely beating of his heart the only sound in the darkness.

He became aware that Edie had come to stand behind Sam. Her eyes were dark pools of sympathy and understanding—for Sam, of course. She would already know the boy couldn't keep the pup, which sent a surge of protective indignation through him. She had really gone too far this time in her quest to "help" his son.

He honestly wondered if he would be able to control his anger at her for putting him in this position.

Holden's gaze returned to his son, who still stood before him with shining eyes. He'd best get this over with quickly.

"You know the town-house complex doesn't allow pets, Sam." He would have given anything not to say these words. "I'm sorry, but you'll have to give the puppy back."

Utter devastation came over the boy as swiftly as it only can in a child. "No! We could keep her. She's not very big. No one would have to know."

"She's only going to get bigger, I assure you," Holden replied, not unkindly. "Anyway, I'm afraid hiding the dog is out of the question. We can't change the rules around to suit us."

He reached down. "Now, let's go ahead and give the puppy back."

"Dad, no!" Sam twisted away, squeezing the animal so tightly it whined. He bent over his precious burden, as if shielding it from harm. "No, please." His voice cracked. "*Please*, Dad."

Holden had never seen Sam this way. Desperate, frantic. He looked around for help and spied two older women standing off to one side, one of whom had to be Olive and the owner of this dog. But neither seemed prompted to take her share of responsibility here.

Except for Edie. She stepped forward, her hair glowing red-gold as it moved around her, her hands gently grasping Sam's shoulders from behind, her eyes downcast, her mouth sad. "Come on, champ. You know your father would let you keep Beauty if he could. Let's give the puppy back to Olive."

Beyond words, the boy shook his head violently.

She pulled Sam back against her, resisting his attempts to shake her off, the curtain of her hair flowing around them both now. "It's okay," she murmured, herself sounding close to tears. "You can come visit her, I promise—"

"No!" Holden snapped. "No more promises, do you hear?"

Her eyes flashed up at him at that, but she held her tongue.

Holden crouched in front of Sam, feeling a little desperate himself. "Come on, son. I wish it were different, but we can't take her with us—"

"No, you don't!" Sam contradicted angrily. "Y-you don't wish it was different! You don't want me to be happy."

A direct hit to the gut, that one was. Holden withstood the buffeting, but just barely. "Sam, this is ridiculous. I refuse to give in to this kind of behavior."

"Oh, all right!" With a strangled sob, Sam shoved Beauty at his father, now acting as if he couldn't be rid of her soon enough. Holden was forced to take the puppy or let it drop to the ground.

Beauty, no canine slacker, zeroed in on the tension in the air. She writhed like a corkscrew in his arms so he thought he almost *would* drop her.

"Hold on, girl, just calm down." Catching a paw under the

chin, he grunted. "For Pete's sake, nobody's going to hurt you."

The dog evidently had no confidence in his character, for that's when she piddled down the front of his white oxford shirt.

Holden held the puppy up and out from him, but the damage was already done. He looked down at the darkened spot on his shirtfront in disgust.

"Why, you little—" His eyes lifted and he found himself nose to shiny black nose with the roly-poly pup and looking straight into her brown eyes.

He blinked. She blinked. The moment was suspended. Then a tiny pink tongue sneaked out for one tentative, conciliatory lick.

Suddenly a thousand good memories flooded through Holden. Memories of laughter and joy and a pair of fine brown eyes....

But along with the good, the pain came, too, as it would be forever mingled in the whole of his life; there was no way to separate the strands of emotion, to choose to keep the best and discard the rest.

Holden realized that, and not the rules, was what had fueled his refusal. He couldn't bear to contemplate Sam enduring more of the pain after all the boy had been through, which came with taking a chance on loving—and losing—again.

Beauty gazed at him, willow-switch tail wagging uncertainly.

Abruptly, Holden felt himself standing back at that crossroads, peering down one path then the other, neither clear, neither guaranteeing a sure thing. And he needed a sure thing right now, urgently, for Sam.

He glanced up at Edie. She stood immobile, sculpted from stone, as if keeping herself from giving even the slightest flinch that might distract him or influence him. Nothing could restrain that cascade of rich copper from coming alive, even in the muffled light, nor banish the deep glow of trust and support reaching out to him from her brown eyes.

Somehow, it was just what he needed to take that first step, although he was no more certain than a moment ago that the direction he headed in was the right one.

"I've been thinking," Holden said, swiping his licked nose against the sleeve of his shirt while continuing to hold the puppy in front of him like a two-fisted hoagie. He wasn't taking a chance on another soaking. "That town house was never meant to be a permanent home. It's probably past time for us to start looking at places where a boy—and a dog— would have some room to play."

Sam, who'd been standing stiff and tense in front of Edie, whipped his chin up and stared at his father.

"You mean...?" Sam asked, his voice filled with a hope and longing that nearly undid Holden. He steeled himself against an overwhelming tide of emotion. He still didn't know if this was the right thing to do, but he saw no way back from this point in time. He had no choice but to go forward.

"You've got yourself a pup, Sam," he said.

The boy's eyes nearly popped out of his head. He threw himself against Holden, hugging him around the waist. "Thanks, Dad!"

A warmth stole through him, slow and sweet and steady.

He handed the pup to Sam, who enfolded her in his arms with a quiet bliss, talking to her soothingly as he practically floated over to where the two women waited to congratulate him on his new pet.

"How about if Beauty remains here," Edie suggested, "where Sam can come and see her regularly, until after you've found a place to live that'll accommodate a dog."

"That makes sense." He ran a hand over the back of his neck. "I'm not that keen a judge of pedigrees, but that looked like a purebred black labrador. Am I right?"

"Yes."

"Well, in that case, introduce me to this Olive so I can write a check for the damage. You wouldn't happen to know if she'll bargain, would you? After all, this whole deal is likely to cost me a bundle when you add in real estate fees, a down payment and moving costs."

Edie laughed, and he realized he liked that sound, too, almost as much as Sam's laughter. "Oh, something tells me if you turn on that charm of yours with Olive, you should be able to shave a few dollars off the price."

His charm? Holden looked at her askance and saw her actually blush. She ducked her head as she shifted on her feet. "I apologize, Dr. McKee, for putting you into that predicament. I honestly had no idea my introducing Sam to the puppy would produce such a reaction in him. You have every right to be angry with me."

"Yes, well." He observed Sam playing with the puppy, already enticing her into a tug of war with a stick he held with the hand that had been injured. The trauma of a few minutes ago seemed completely forgotten.

"Kids sure do know how to hit you where you live, don't they?" Holden said abruptly.

"How do you mean?" Edie asked.

"I mean, I can know it intellectually that Sam doesn't really believe I don't want him to be happy. But when you get hit with it, man, it's no fun. It felt like a knife in my gut." The admission had come from him before he'd had a chance to think.

He made as if to leave "Well," he said stiffly, "we should be going."

"Oh, but I feel like the least I can do to make up for your trouble is to ask you to stay for supper," she said on a quick rush of air.

One eyebrow lifting, Holden looked at her. Under his scrutiny, her skin flushed across the cheekbones in a most appealing fashion. She looked almost poised for flight after making her offer, and Holden realized Sam was not the only one he feared would get hurt by life and love.

Or by him. He couldn't give her what she needed.

Then a slight breeze sent her hair adrift, gossamer strands streaming across her face. Edie brushed them back in a gesture he found abruptly sensual. He remembered the moment when *he* had made that gesture and how it had felt—like the forging of a wide river that, once begun, would be impossible to turn back from.

His heart thudded out a caution, but for the first time in a long time he chose to ignore the warning. The pull was too strong. His own need was too strong.

"I never turn down a home-cooked meal," Holden assured her.

"Coffee?" Edie asked, pushing open the screen door with her elbow, two steaming mugs in her hands.

Holden straightened from where he'd been leaning a shoulder against the colonnade and turned. "Sure."

He took a mug from her and carefully settled on the wide porch rail. Edie chose a seat on the porch swing a few yards away.

It was that perfect time of year when it was warm without being too warm, and the mosquitoes had yet to hatch. That didn't stop every other manner of moth and bug from flitting madly around the porch light, their frenzied gyrations casting points of shadow that swirled and circled like the speckles inside a crystal snow-making ball.

Edie studied Holden covertly over the rim of her coffee cup. He'd been rather pensive throughout supper, and she'd found herself attuned to his every movement and word, as if looking for a sign of some kind. She still hadn't had time to completely absorb the realization that he was the boy in her visions, for lack of a better term. She couldn't believe them to be anything more than flashes from her subconscious that fell between dreaming and intuition.

If so, what was her subconscious mind trying to tell her? What did she want in such a deep-down way it was beyond conscious thought?

At least she knew this: she wanted to help Holden McKee. She'd witnessed a breakthrough this evening, when a small chink of metal had fallen from his personal armor. Edie would never forget the look on his face as he held that puppy. It had sent a thrill through her that still resonated and made her quiver.

Yes, perhaps there *was* hope for him yet.

"Hazel took Sam over to Olive's to say good-night to Beauty," Edie blurted out, for want of anything better to say.

Holden glanced up. "That's good," he said absently.

He'd changed out of his stained shirt to a clean one he happened to have in some workout gear in his car. The black T-shirt fit him well. Very well. She hadn't realized how broad his shoulders were, how well-defined the muscles in his arms and torso. Or perhaps she had, and hadn't felt it safe to acknowledge her notice of him in that way.

That quiver intensified, like a candle flame flickering in the breeze.

"Oh! Umph, ow," Edie exclaimed, having inattentively taken a large gulp of hot coffee.

"You okay?"

"Yes." Disgusted with herself, she wiped a dribble off her chin. This sure was her day for accidents. Her biorhythms were all probably on a downward course, that's what it was.

"Your aunt's condition," Holden said abruptly. "Rheumatoid arthritis?"

Peering at him as he studied the contents of his cup, elbows on his thighs, Edie wondered at the choice of subject but answered him readily enough. "Yes."

He took a quick swallow of his coffee, still scrutinizing it as if it contained the answer to some puzzle. "And you take care of her?"

"Don't let her hear you say that," she said on a chuckle. "I help her out, yes, but Aunt Hazel gets around pretty well for a sixty-nine-year-old with such a painful disease."

"Is it the same degenerative disease you mentioned your mother had?"

"No." She drew her knees up to her chest and hugged them. "I know rheumatoid arthritis can run in families, but that wasn't the case here. They were sisters, though, Mom the younger by a year."

"Really?" Holden frowned, finally glancing up. "I wouldn't place any bets on your age, but wouldn't that have made your mother well into her forties when she had you?"

Edie rubbed an index finger across her chin as it rested on her hands. "She had me on her forty-fifth birthday—December 20."

He frowned even harder as he stared at her.

"What?" Edie asked, sitting up straight, a tingle of alarm skittering across the back of her shoulders.

"What on earth happened to your knees?"

"Oh, that!" Flashes of her vision whisked past her mind's eye. "I...I fell down today when Sam and I were taking a walk. I mean, I was running." She gave a nervous laugh. "Really hit the dirt, too."

"It looks like it." Before she could react, Holden was beside her on the swing, come to get a closer look. "Nasty-looking bruising. Did you thoroughly wash the scrapes and treat them with antiseptic?"

"Of course."

"Good. Any swelling around the patella?"

He reached out, intending to palpate the site, Edie was sure, but she wasn't about to wait for confirmation. She was up and off the swing and halfway across the porch in an instant.

"Really, Dr. McKee," she said rather breathlessly, her back

to him. "I know how to evaluate an injury and administer simple first aid."

"Call me Holden."

"Only if you stop treating me like one of your patients," she retorted with a dash of impatience, though she couldn't have said where it came from.

There was a pause, and then Holden said softly, "Yes, you're quite good at nursing any number of hurts, aches and pains—especially of others. Although Olive did make some oblique comment to me that if you weren't free to give her a massage, was the doctor making house calls this evening?"

Edie was surprised into laughter. "I swear, she's shameless!"

It was just enough of a break in the tension that she could turn around and ask, "Why all the questions about me?"

He'd come to his feet sometime when her back had been to him and stood with his hands in his trouser pockets. The light from the yellow bug-deterring bulb washed out any colors, so that not only Holden's shirt but also his hair and eyes were black, his skin and lips sepia-toned, his face sapped of any expression. Or perhaps the last wasn't caused by the light.

"You're very good with Sam, you know," he said, somewhat grudgingly. "I wanted to let you know I appreciate the attention and care you've shown him."

"It's been entirely my pleasure. He's a very sweet boy."

"I know." He sighed. "He's going through a rough time right now."

"You're both going through a rough time, Holden," she corrected him gently.

He pivoted a half turn to send his gaze out to search the night beyond the circle of light, his profile clear-cut and somber. "I should explain my reaction to the puppy. You see, I had a dog when I was his age, when I still lived in East Texas."

Edie cocked her head, for some reason compelled to listen very hard at that moment. "You did?"

"Yeah." He dropped his chin with a private smile, shaking his head slightly. "She was...something else. She'd been given to my father when she was just a pup as payment for his services. Around those parts, that's a hefty compensation considering how people prize a good hunting dog."

Edie nodded in understanding, her spirits unaccountably buoyed. It was probably because he was opening up to her a little. She would have to make sure any support or advice she gave was soft-shoed. "What did your father do?"

The smile died. "He was a GP. A rural doctor."

"I gather he's why you decided to go into medicine?"

"No," Holden said definitely, then gave a short, soundless chuckle. "No, I can't say as he had a whole lot of influence over me, since he died when I was eight." He slanted her a glance. "He was more like you, someone who tried to minister to his patients' every need. In fact, that's how he died. An influenza outbreak had taken down half the county. Twenty-three were gone by the time it was all over, my father one of them."

"I'm...I'm so sorry," she said, feeling the sympathy as inadequate now as she had when she'd given it in response to the news about his wife's passing.

Edie pulled the braid she'd put her hair into over her shoulder, fingering its silky tail in an automatic gesture of security. "It must have been very hard for you and the rest of your family."

"There was just me and my mother." A frog croaked close by, another answered from farther away. "She died a few years after my father passed on."

"Oh, *Holden*," Edie murmured, a familiar picture beginning to form in her mind, one very close to her own heart. "How alone in the world you must have felt!"

He lifted one shoulder, a dismissive gesture that didn't at

all fool Edie. "I believe my mother would have done anything not to have to leave me, which I think has helped me through the years. But in the end...she wanted to go. She missed him," he said quietly. "I just wanted her pain and suffering to end."

"I-I know." Yes, she knew how it was to let someone go to be with another, to be the one left behind.

"The real blow, though," he went on, "was that same day—the day my mother died—I also lost...her. My dog. She saved my life—and I failed to return the favor. It was because of my foolish wish to go after something I wanted to take with me that caused her death. At the time, I knew it would have meant risking my life to try and save her. But I think if I'd have known how alone I'd feel after she died, I would have done it, no matter the risk."

Edie stared at him, her heart wrenching so hard in her chest the pain brought tears to her eyes. It did seem the crowning blow, and all she could see before her was the boy he'd been standing alone, so alone it echoed across time.

Head still down, Holden stood motionless, as if in prayer. But that was apparently the furthest thing from his mind, for next he said into the hushed air, "I think the day I lost Elsa was the day I stopped believing in there being any master plan, any meaning to life. The last time I let myself really care..."

He shook his head, as if chasing the thoughts from it.

Yes, Edie saw him clearly as he must have been then, so much like Sam, forlorn, friendless and confused. Yet it was the Holden before her now who drew on the deepest of her emotions. Even though she understood now how the loss of his wife would have reignited in him long, smoldering childhood fears of being left behind, what again stirred up in her that sense of impending danger was seeing him as one who felt abandoned by everyone he'd ever loved—and that he felt there was no point in trying to learn to love again without them.

In the next moment he confirmed her fears.

"If anything," Holden continued on with a strange detachment, "it's because of my mother that I went into medicine. I always regretted not being able to have done more for her. Maybe, in some way, I was trying to rewrite the past. Or to still make sense of it. Or to keep on trying to be happy. But then when Sam's mother was struck down with no warning or reason...I just thought, hell, what's the use?"

Edie took three urgent steps toward him. "You couldn't have prevented their deaths, Holden. You aren't God."

He cocked that infernally skeptical eyebrow at her. "Yes, but as you recall, I don't believe there's an all-powerful being who cares enough to look out for us."

"So you've said, as well as believing there's no meaning to anything that happens. According to you, we're all just hurtling through space on a random trajectory!"

He crossed his arms, no longer distant. "How well put."

She set her hands on her hips. "Then let me ask you this, Dr. McKee—why is it you do what you do? Why continue to be a physician and try to save people's lives? Why try to be a good parent to Sam? Why even try to go on at all if you feel there's nothing to live for anymore since your wife died?"

She spread the fingers of one hand on her chest. "Goodness, I can imagine what you must think of me for having any kind of trust in the world or for caring for the people in it, including your son!"

"I'm not you, all right?" Holden exploded, closing the space between them, the force of him towering over her. She held her ground fearlessly. "I can't go around promising people that things'll turn out when I don't have any assurance they will!"

His face had drained of all color, this time from no trick of the light, Edie knew. "And I'm *definitely* not like my father. I mean, correct me if I'm wrong, but I don't recall anything in the Hippocratic oath that calls for me to sacrifice my life for another!"

She looked up at him, her heart rent in two at his grief and anguish. "No one's asked you to, Holden," she said quietly.

At that, he blinked rapidly, as if he were coming out of a trance.

"No," he finally said, his voice no longer filled with pain and anger. "You're right. No one's asked that of me. And believe it or not, sometimes I wonder why."

He turned away from her then and stopped at the edge of the porch, where he leaned upon one outstretched arm braced against the round colonnade, his head flung back as he scrutinized the night sky as if to find there some answer to the questions in his life.

Edie watched him, knowing he would find no answers, not there. She'd already searched the stars and the heavens herself, and it had all come down to a single understanding: sometimes you just had to let go of having to know and keep on living— and loving—to the best of your ability, with the belief the answers would come in good time.

But there was no way to bring a person to such an understanding if he wasn't open to trusting. And she had no earthly idea of what she could do to help bring Holden to that point in his thinking. She'd seen how her father had given up after losing her mother, and from what Holden had just told her, his mother had been the same way. She didn't want to think what had happened to them would happen to Holden. Perhaps that was part of what she was scared about for him.

Tears stung in her eyes. She didn't want to stop believing he'd come around. But she didn't know what else to do.

Except offer him some small comfort in the form of a simple touch, just to say *you're not alone*.

Stealing up behind Holden, Edie lifted her hand...and hesitated at the sight of that immutable, solid back of his. It seemed a brick wall; no chance of it yielding. No chance of making an impression. Was she foolish for trying?

Tentatively, she laid her hand upon his shoulder.

To Edie's surprise, her touch did seem to set off a reaction in Holden. He spun around, startling a gasp out of her as he grabbed her upper arms, his chest bumping up against hers.

"Stop it!" he ordered. "Just stop it, all right?"

Edie barely heard him, so great was the shock of that contact. It tore through her like a spark along a fuse.

"Stop what?" she asked, thoroughly disoriented.

"I'm not one of *your* patients, either, Edie! And I'm definitely not a little boy with a broken wing. Platitudes and encouraging pats on the back are not what I need from you."

She shook her head, trying to clear it as she drew in a shuddering breath, which brought her breasts flush up against him.

She saw the havoc her action wreaked on his composure. On his ability to remain detached and in control, which was so blasted important to him, and not just as a physician.

Fully knowing what she was doing, she took another lung-filling breath. His gaze burned into hers, warning her of the fire raging within him.

Edie didn't pull away. Couldn't turn away, and not because she had promised herself she wouldn't.

"What *do* you need from me, then?" she asked.

The fire glowed brighter, consuming him. Consuming her.

"This," Holden muttered. And his mouth came down on hers in a kiss of explosive force.

She felt it go off inside her as her lips parted under his and he found the moist, warm center of her with his tongue. Her knees nearly buckled, and she clutched his shoulders as one of his arms went around her waist, his other hand supporting the back of her head as he took the kiss deeper, as deep as it would go.

This was why she'd been afraid of touching him. Not because she'd get no response, but because she'd been afraid of setting off this eruption of passion in both of them. The passion, and the need that pulled her toward him, into him and his own need of her. Yes, she had chosen to see him as a doctor or a parent or a person—anything but as a man who could awaken the most womanly part of her, beyond maternal instincts, beyond her nurturing nature. Because all aspects of her womanhood started right here, with this link between a woman and a man.

"You put your hair back," he growled against her mouth, and she realized his fingers tugged at her braid.

"It...it sometimes gets in the way."

"Now's not one of those times."

She heard the covered rubber band slide to the porch floor, then lost herself in the sensation of him unplaiting her hair with a swift urgency. Her hands came up to touch him as fervently, fingers spreading across the flat planes of his roughened jaw and cheeks. They scraped the tender skin of her palms, but she didn't care as she sent her hands creeping up to his temples to lose themselves in the thicket of his hair.

She felt as if she were becoming unraveled as well as he completed his handiwork and spread the heavy mass of hair around her shoulders, around them.

He made a low sound of satisfaction.

Within their cocoon, Edie wrapped her arms around his neck, pressing closer to him, and Holden grasped her hips, helping her, as his mouth continued its onslaught, pursuing a trail down her jaw, over the sensitive skin of her throat, then back up to take the tender lobe of her ear between his teeth, nipping it gently.

Edie gasped as millions of sensations she'd never felt before multiplied a thousand times over within a heartbeat and completely overran any thought but to sigh his name over and over, as if to make up for all the times she had held back from saying it.

"Why," Holden murmured hotly into her ear, "do I have this persistent feeling you've been put in my path either to torment me or...or I don't know what."

She shook her head mutely, causing his lips to brush against the skin just below the hairline at her nape, and sending another thrill coursing through her. But she couldn't have said why he had been brought into her life, either. He confused her, raised such conflicting feelings in her.

Then there was that danger for him springing from her visions. It confused her, too, made her afraid. She was so scared if he were allowed to, he'd give up. Wasn't that part of what she'd seen in that boyish face in those visions? What had she shouted at him?

No! Don't do it! Don't you dare give—

But it wasn't she who'd said that. It had been Holden. And suddenly Edie knew, in a streak of precognition: the danger was not for him. It was for her.

She stiffened involuntarily, bewilderment and fear a-riot in her brain. Holden stilled as well, then shook his head as if to clear it.

"I'm scaring you," he said, his breath ragged against her throat, and for a moment he seemed to hold her closer, as if seeking to allay her panic. "I'm...I'm sorry. I didn't mean for this to happen. I shouldn't have wanted so much—"

He let her go then, almost pushing her from him. Edie stumbled backward a few steps, her arm shooting out to catch her balance on the rail. Holden retreated as well, and suddenly there was a gap of five feet between them where seconds before there had been none. She felt both incredibly cheated of his nearness and lucky to have escaped some disaster at the same time.

She was trembling uncontrollably, goose bumps spreading in countless pinpricks all over her skin. Edie clutched her elbows in her hands, her forearms pressed against her middle, to try to stop them.

Hazarding a glance at Holden, she saw that he, too, was disturbed. His face drawn, he ran unsteady fingers through his hair. He noted her stance, half turned from him, and his eyes grew dark and urgent.

"Edie, please," he said, voice low and pleading, holding a hand out to her. "Please, don't give up on—"

"Well, Beauty's all fed and watered and petted within an inch of her life and tucked in to bed," Hazel announced as she and Sam came around the side of the house. She stopped immediately upon spotting the two tense figures standing on opposite sides of the porch. Sam came up short beside her, his gaze puzzled.

Scrambling to pull her wits together, Edie forced a strained smile. "Sounds like she'll be fine until you can come back to see her, doesn't it, Sam?"

"Yeah, I think so," he answered, a little dubiously. He turned to his father. "When *can* we come back, Dad? Tomorrow night?"

Holden cleared his throat. "I don't think we can make it as soon as that, son. I've got a couple of meetings coming up the next few evenings. We need to check with Olive to find out when's convenient for her, too."

"But couldn't I just come home with Edie again, like I did tonight?" Sam asked.

"We need to be considerate of other people's time."

"But Beauty'll forget all about me! What if we took her with us, just for one night—"

"Sam." Holden's tone brooked no argument. "I know you're anxious to see Beauty again as soon as possible, but you knew when we made this arrangement that you would need to trust the puppy's care to others for a while. I don't intend to haggle with you about it."

Sam's lower lip looked like it might make a rebel stand, but then the boy nodded resignedly. "All right."

Edie stepped forward. "I'll give you a full report on Beauty when you come for your appointment on Thursday, okay,

Sam? If Olive doesn't have a photo of her, I'll take a picture so you'll have something to keep with you."

Sam brightened. "Would you?"

"Of course," she said warmly. Belatedly, she remembered Holden's admonishment of making no more promises. Venturing a look at him, she saw his eyebrows had lowered, shielding the expression in his eyes.

He was back to his old closed-off self. She felt very empty inside.

"Time to go home, Sam." Holden crossed the porch and descended the steps to take his son's hand. He nodded toward Hazel. "Thank you for dinner. It was very good."

"Don't thank me, Doctor," Hazel said, a trifle defiantly. "Edie does most of the cooking in this house, especially when my arthritis makes it so I can barely grasp a vegetable peeler."

That wasn't strictly true, Edie thought, but didn't correct her, as Holden turned to her and said stiffly, although not ungraciously, "Then thank you, Edie."

"You're welcome, Holden," she murmured to his back, since he hadn't waited for her reply but strode off, Sam in tow, into the shadows of the night, as if he couldn't wait to quit her.

Still, Edie stood steadfast, waiting until Holden had loaded Sam into their car and had driven away, their taillights two embers glowing in the dark, because she had vowed she wouldn't turn away.

But she hadn't dreamed how hard it would prove to keep that promise.

Chapter Six

"Dr. McKee!"

Holden turned, spying a vaguely familiar man who came hurrying toward him down the hospital corridor, a blond-haired woman in tow. The look on her face was somewhat bewildered, but the man was all smiles.

He stopped in front of Holden and took a moment to catch his breath. "I'm glad I caught you. Terry and I had come to our first cardiac education class on the other side of the hospital, and I thought, shoot, as long as we're here, let's see if we can find the man responsible for this whole new kick we're on."

A light clicked on in Holden's brain. "Oh, yes, you're—"

"Andy Osgood—with the chest pains a few weeks ago. This is my wife, Terry." The man looked florid not so much with exertion as excitement. "I just really needed to thank you, Doctor. After you gave me that lecture, I went home and had a long talk with Terry here, and she said everything you did. That life is precious, and I can't live in fear of what might happen or what already happened, like with my dad dying so early. Terry and the kids deserve better than a guy who holds himself back from giving all he can to them today just because he's scared of what might come tomorrow."

He took his wife's hand in his, and she smiled up at him with a look of pure love. "We've made some changes. Terry got a part-time job doing accounting, which'll keep her current in her field, and so I won't feel so much pressure in case something *does* happen to me. We're socking that extra money into savings. And we're spending more time together. Sometimes that means walking out of work when six people are screaming for a report that was due yesterday, but what's a guy to do? I'm not married to my job."

"That's right," Terry piped up. "You're married to *me,* and don't you forget it."

They laughed, and Holden found himself smiling at their obvious happiness. "Well, I'm glad for you," he said. "You're one of the lucky ones, Mr. Osgood. You got your wake-up call pretty early in the game, you know? You paid attention to it, that's the main thing."

Osgood gave him a chagrined look. "Yeah, well, you were kind of hard to ignore when you got into my face like that."

Holden's own conscience goaded him. "Actually, I should apologize for—"

Osgood held up a hand. "No, don't apologize, Doctor. You took the time to care about what happened to me. As frustrating as it probably is for you to see ten guys like me continue to self-destruct, I hope it's worth it when someone does listen."

Andy Osgood's rather ordinary face suddenly became suffused with an inner inspiration that made him over into a man of conviction. "In a way," he added, "you rescued me. I guess you could say I owe you my life, Dr. McKee."

He shook Holden's hand another time, his gratefulness obviously heartfelt and sincere, then stepped back with a nod. "Well, we won't keep you. I know you're busy."

"Not at all," Holden replied, meaning it. He would never be too busy to listen to such a testimonial.

After the Osgoods had gone on their way, he moved to one side of the corridor to let a gurney go by, and became suddenly lost in thought.

Andy Osgood believed he'd saved his life. Often Holden *had* saved lives: He'd held a beating heart in his hands, had cleared an airway so that life-giving air could fill a set of lungs. Had worked with fevered purpose to save a newborn.

But this was different. This was making a unique kind of difference in people's lives, one that handed the responsibility—and control—for their well-being back to them, setting them free to go on and make a difference in others' lives.

Because he wasn't God.

Granted, he didn't always have to bawl some guy out to get him to wake up and smell the coffee, Holden thought wryly. Still, he could do something proactive instead of reactive to help people, to make a difference, to change the world. Don't wait until the damage is done, the fire started, to come in and put it out. That was the easy way out—in those cases, almost any effort was deemed helpful, any failures excused by the urgency of the circumstances. Instead, why not become more involved in caring not merely physically for a patient but emotionally?

Rather than try to prevent them from having to feel more pain, why not give them the support they need to cope with the changes and losses that are a part of life?

Holden knew this was how his father had thought, what he believed was his role as a doctor. Such a philosophy was certainly more along the lines of Edie's approach, what she considered her responsibility in her work—indeed, in her life.

Yes, Edie. Closing his eyes, Holden leaned his head back against the wall, his mind's eye filled with the look of her.

She really was very pretty in a wholesome, natural way, not a freckle marring that creamy complexion. In stark contrast, her lashes were the color of cinnamon stick. And curly. Then there was her mouth...

Here, his inner gaze lingered on her full lower lip, the upper one deeply bowed in the middle. He didn't think he'd noticed that enticing indentation before, though he couldn't have said why. Perhaps because he hadn't allowed himself to think of her that way on the whole, as an attractive, sensual woman. Or because he'd been afraid to look at her that way, suspecting he would want more.

She had quite simply gotten to him, at first wending her way into his thoughts, then seeming to influence his actions— as if her light touch rested on the back of his hand in all that he did. He'd found himself wondering if she could be taking root in his heart.

The possibility scared the hell out of him.

Yet he wouldn't trade for all the gold in the world the experience of feeling her response to his caresses and kisses. For one brief, singular moment she had held nothing back from him of herself, not of her heart or soul or body. He'd found himself so needful of that response from her, needed it in *his* heart and soul and body. It was almost as if they'd been yearning toward that connection for a time out of dimension...

Before she pulled back.

He wondered why she had—hell, he'd lain awake for hours trying to figure it out. Cursed himself for frightening her with the intensity of his need to erase any gap between them. Yet for all his trying, he hadn't been able to close it. And it was because *he* had held back from meeting her halfway.

That, more than anything, was what he grappled with during some very long, sleepless nights. It was one thing to have a change of heart about how he dealt with his patients. But to open himself up to trust another to hold *his* heart completely in her hands...? He couldn't believe it would ever happen. How could it? It hadn't happened with Rose, not in seven years of marriage. He had loved her, yes—but had he taken that last step into true and complete love with her? No. He had not. And it was a failing Holden lived with every day.

So it would be best if he just stayed clear of Edie Turner. He didn't want to see her hurt, and that was what he was bound to do to her. He should do everything he could to set her running as hard as she could in the opposite direction from him.

But he knew it was easier said than done, because he wasn't sure he could stop wanting her, wanting from her all she could give....

With a sound of frustration and disgust, he pushed off from the wall and headed down the hallway for the lab, his original destination before he'd been sidetracked by such lines of thought. The truth of the situation was, he wanted all without giving all. He wanted surety. A promise. Well he knew, though, that the world didn't work that way.

So why, then, couldn't he stop wanting so much for it to?

Sam proudly turned his arm every which way for Edie's observation.

"See?" he insisted. "It's all better! I can do almost everything I used to. I don't even need the splint anymore."

"And just in time for summer," Edie agreed, deciding to keep private for the moment any cautions or reservations as to the extent of his recovery. Sam's attitude about his injury had improved three hundred percent since Beauty had come into his life over a week ago, and Edie knew how embracing a positive outlook was half the battle in rehabilitating an injury.

Yet she also knew there was still much healing to be done.

"Yeah, just in time for summer," Sam echoed excitedly. Emotions flitted across his features, lighting his gray eyes and changing them like quicksilver. "I can't wait. I hope me and Dad find a house soon. Did you know Beauty's gained two pounds already? Olive said she's house-trained, but I'm gonna haveta teach her to sit and lie down and fetch and heel myself. Dad said he can help me with that. He had a dog when he was a boy like me, did you know?"

"Y-yes," Edie stammered, the pervading trepidation she'd battled over the past week slipping up on her again. It came upon her whenever thoughts of Holden sneaked past her defenses, which happened more often than she was finding almost able to endure.

She changed the subject before Sam had a chance to chatter on about his father. "Will you do me a favor, Sam? I know you're excited to be getting back to normal again, but will you try to be aware of your healing arm, take it easy still?"

Sam's look of skepticism was a miniature image of his father's.

So she wasn't to escape reminders of Holden today. However, this boy, and not his father, was her primary concern right now.

Propping her hands on either side of him as he sat on the examining table, Edie bent to eye level with Sam. "Remember when you agreed to trust me, champ?"

He paused, then nodded solemnly.

"I know it looks and feels as if your arm is all better, but it's still got some mending to do inside the joint with the bones and the tendons." She took his forearm in her hands, fingers palpating the site to show him where she meant. "It's like...like how you'll be expected to take care of Beauty. She's doesn't know her limits yet, and you're in charge of making sure she doesn't overdo it, keeping her busy with games she can handle and that help her to grow and get strong a little at a time. Does that make sense?"

"Yeah," Sam said, a kind of quiet amazement in his voice, "it does."

"Good. And I'd like you still to wear the splint when you're playing with Beauty, just for one week more. It'll help support your forearm just in case you were to strain it by accident."

He almost looked as if he would argue that point with her, but Edie could see his mind working, going over all that she had ever told him or done for him, and coming up with a winning record so far.

"Okay, Edie," he agreed at last. "I'll be careful."

She gave his arm a gentle squeeze and let go, although he no longer shied from her touch. On the contrary, Edie discovered it was she who was reluctant to establish any stronger tie to this child than she already had.

She couldn't put off any longer what she knew must come.

"Well, Sam," she said with a false cheerfulness she hoped the boy wouldn't detect. "Looks like we're through for today. I'm going to have Colleen take you to the exercise area so you can do your time with the rebounder while I have a word with your father."

She helped the boy down and accompanied him to front desk, where her aide was ready for him. Seeing Sam off, Edie turned and found Holden watching her as he sat in one of the chairs in a bank lining the wall.

Their gazes locked, and all of her unexplainable apprehensions from the evening of their kiss came flooding back, almost as quickly as did the rush of remembered yearning she'd experienced in his arms.

She would have to learn Holden's technique of detaching himself emotionally from a situation. It certainly had its uses.

Praying her reaction didn't show on her face, Edie indicated one of the open treatment rooms. "If you have a moment..."

Holden immediately stood. "Sure."

Once inside the room, Edie closed the door behind her, recalling another time when she'd asked to see this man privately, how his son's welfare had been foremost in her mind, and how she'd been afraid but that it hadn't been anything she'd not felt capable of handling.

Now, though, she found herself nearly trembling. She headed for the other side of the room and rounded the far side of the treatment table, needing to put both distance and substance between herself and this man.

It was he who spoke first. "I think I've found the right house for Sam and me."

She looked around in surprise. "Really? Why...that's wonderful!"

He flashed a quick smile. "It's on the north side of the metroplex past the end of the Dallas tollway, which means a pretty smooth commute to the hospital. It's an older home, too, not one of the new constructions that have been going up in those parts, on a big fenced lot with mature trees, two of them pecans."

"That'll be fun, come autumn, shelling your own pecan crop."

"I was thinking that, too." He leaned a shoulder against the wall, hands thrust deeply into his trouser pockets. "Oh, and it's within walking distance of Sam's new school. I've met the neighbors, too. They have a seven-year-old boy. The wife works from their house, and she's happy to make both Sam and Beauty a part of their home when I'm working."

He frowned in thought. "We won't be moving until the end of the month, I'm afraid, which means I'll have to impose on Olive to keep Beauty for a few more weeks, if that's all right."

"Oh, I don't need to talk to Olive to know she feels you haven't imposed one bit. Sh-she'll miss seeing Sam once he takes Beauty to your new home."

Edie heard her voice grow rough with emotion, knowing what was to come, and paused to clear her throat. It wouldn't be like this forever, she desperately assured herself.

"The house sounds perfect for you," she said, forcing a smile. Truly, she was thrilled for them both.

Holden seemed pleased, too. Chin down, he shook his head. "Yeah, it seems like the place was just waiting for me to go looking for it."

He glanced up from under those expressive eyebrows of his.

"I have you to thank for suggesting the move, Edie. I don't know how you do it, but you just seem to know what I...what's needed."

Edie felt her face turn hot with an almost guilty pleasure, which she hid with the fall of her hair over her shoulder as she placed Sam's file on the leatherette surface. "Please, I can't take credit for what you'd have seen yourself before too much longer."

"Would I have?" Holden asked.

"Of course." Finding herself growing uncomfortable with this tack in the conversation, Edie swung it back on course. "Well, I'm happy to say I have more good news for you. I think I'll be able to release Sam from regular PT after the next appointment."

Holden straightened. "So soon?"

Was it her imagination or did she hear disappointment in his voice?

Edie flipped Sam's file open on the table and perused its contents with undue attention. "You know, naturally, that he passed his recheck with his orthopedist with flying colors. He's reached all of his identified goals. Functional use and mobility are at nearly one hundred percent."

Goodness, she sounded like Holden in his most reserved doctor-knows-best mode!

Which prompted the physician in him to cross the room and come around the edge of the table to have a look at Sam's file himself. The problem was, that brought him within a breath of her as he leaned over her shoulder.

"Yes, I see," he said musingly. "But what's your opinion about Sam's progress psychologically dealing with his injury?"

"He's come a long way there, too. I'm sure you've seen the strides he's made in the past ten days alone, although the credit for that has to go to Beauty."

He set his hand on the tabletop next to hers. "I've got to give you credit for that, too, for bringing the pup into his life."

"Yes. Well." Edie slapped Sam's file shut and sidestepped away from the circle of warmth emanating from Holden. "In any case, Sam's clearly on the way to recovery and ready to go it on his own—with your help, of course. Certainly, we could continue having him come here to do his exercises, but I know you'll see that he keeps them up for the next month."

"Really?" Holden took back the step she'd set between them, so that Edie was compelled to meet his eyes. "Are you saying that you...trust me, Edie?" he asked, his voice deep and resonant. She felt it vibrate all the way down to her toes.

His gaze searched hers. She held her ground, but just barely. *Did* she trust him? And if not, why? Or did she really want to know?

She hated that she would even come close to shying from the truth. It wasn't her. She wasn't the sort of person who lived in a state of doubt, almost as if she feared discovery. Or was it in fear of what she might discover—about herself or Holden?

Edie closed her eyes and concentrated, tried to get back to the heart of the matter, the heart of herself. She mustn't turn away now, must be strong—for Sam's sake.

"Yes," she said, answering Holden's question. She opened her eyes and looked at him straight on, adding significantly, "Where your son's concerned, I do trust you, Dr. McKee."

She couldn't call him Holden, not in this setting, not when doing so would call up when she'd last said it aloud, his name a mantra on her lips, as she'd been lost in his embrace.

His dark lashes flickered, as if a pang of pain had passed through him. "I see."

She felt a stab to her own heart for him. She didn't want to hurt him, but she had to be honest, must continue to be so.

"Keeping Sam up with his exercises is only part of what you'll be dealing with, Doctor," Edie said, making herself go on. "You see, he's getting his confidence back, which means he'll quickly and conveniently forget his arm is still on the mend. Now, he's promised me he'll be mindful, but you'll have to keep an eye on him and—unfortunately—be prepared to be cast again in the role of the big, bad, mean dad."

"I'll handle it." His gaze didn't waver an iota this time, making her hesitate.

She had to press forward, however, although now it was for both Holden's and Sam's welfare. "Sam may seem to be completely healed emotionally, too. But he still has much to resolve, and not just with regard to his injury."

The muscle in his jaw leapt. "I know that."

"Yes, I believe you do know that," she said gently. "Still, it's going to be tough not to shove any lingering issues under the carpet. It's human nature to do so, but you'll have to be strong."

"And I'm only human, is that what you're saying?"

"I'm not criticizing you or attacking you or even looking for a debate, Doctor, honestly, I'm not. I'm just saying that it's going to be hard to keep to the heart of the matter, because when our immediate crisis of spirit is past, we're quick to grab onto anything but trust to attach our hopes to. And the more we count on such false foundations of security, the harder it is to let them go again and simply...believe."

She knew her emotions showed on her face. "Believe it or not, it's almost easier to remain trustful when you've got nowhere else to go but forward, and nothing to go there on but that trust—and love. Love, of course, is the bridge."

Edie waited for him to get up in arms, as he did whenever she pushed him to look inside himself. But not this time. As with his son, she could almost see Holden's mind working as he strove to grasp so ethereal a concept, which went against the grain of his standard mode of thinking as a physician, a scientist, and a man.

No—he was a man first. She wouldn't forget that again.

Couldn't forget it as the moment drew taut, the tension between them sharpening. Edie remembered when it had last been like this, remembered Holden's action as he'd sought answers for his questions by pulling her to him and kissing her. Yet they'd learned nothing, except maybe how truly discordant they were with each other, always facing the other over issues from opposite sides.

"You make it sound like you'll never see me again," Holden said quietly. "Sam, I mean. You promised to be there for him."

"And I have been, but now...my work is done—as his physical therapist, which is, as you once pointed out to me, what I am to him and nothing more. I'm surprised you haven't brought it up again—that I need to keep from getting so emotionally involved with my patients. I've certainly gotten the lecture more than once from my supervisor."

And if she only knew the half of it, she'd reprimand Edie big time.

"Besides, Doctor," Edie added softly, "it's not me Sam needs to be there for him."

He said nothing for a long time. Then he asked, "So I guess what you're saying is, this is goodbye?"

"Yes. Yes, it is." The moment begged for her to extend her hand to him in a goodwill gesture, but she didn't think it would help make it easier for either of them.

Instead Edie pasted a smile on her face that she hoped was bright yet feared was brittle. It certainly felt as if it would crack into a thousand pieces at any second. "I have no doubt you'll do fine on your own. You and Sam."

Holden only nodded, slowly, and turned away.

The ache in her doubled and tripled. She felt as if she was letting him down. As if she was letting herself down.

He stopped, though, pivoting back toward her. "I'm bringing Sam over to Olive's to visit Beauty on Saturday around four," he said. "Will you be around?"

"I really don't know if that's wise—"

"Sam's counting on your being there, you or Hazel. Some promise about him getting up on a horse for the first time?" he asked skeptically.

"Oh, that was only on condition of your wholehearted permission," Edie hastened to explain.

"Should I give it?"

She spread her hands in front of her. "It's up to you. We're not talking about galloping breakneck across a pasture, just a little walk around the yard with the horse on a lead. I can assure you, Sam would be perfectly safe with either me or Hazel, but I'd make sure I was there at first, since Sam's more familiar with me than my aunt, until he got comfortable with the situation."

"That sounds great," Holden agreed, rather quickly for him, Edie thought. She realized why when added, "Because after you've spent time with Sam, maybe *we* could find some time together, too. To...talk, maybe go get a bite to eat, if Olive and Hazel wouldn't mind watching Sam."

It took a second before Edie realized she had just been asked out on a date. He'd maneuvered her into it, quite shamelessly. Yet she knew how hard it had been for him to take that step toward making a connection with her again.

Yes, they *had* made a connection, however briefly, had found it somehow among all the pain and fears and doubts.

As if he knew her thoughts, his gaze grew intense, delving into hers, making a sweet ache for that joining to fill her again.

Edie had to clasp her hands behind her to keep from reaching out to him. Because it wasn't yet right. It wouldn't be completely right until she confronted the fear she felt with him and understood it.

Her vague apprehension returned, this time telling her that seeing him this way wasn't what was best for her. But it also told her she was helpless to deny him, to stop herself from wanting to for herself, even as she knew Holden wouldn't be the only one trying to find answers from without, rather than from within.

"All right, Holden," Edie said. "I'll be there."

Edie didn't turn around when she heard the screen door open and close behind her as she sat on the second step of the front porch and gazed out at the stars. The night sky was especially deep tonight, making her think she might in fact find some profound wisdom there.

Hazel gave a huff as she eased herself down beside Edie, one hand on her niece's shoulder. "Gracious sakes alive, I'm sore tonight!" she exclaimed.

Edie put an arm around her aunt, rubbing one shoulder. "I'm sorry. Would you like a massage and a little TLC tonight?"

Hazel patted her knee. "Actually, I kinda had the notion *you* could use a little care and concern this evening. You barely said a word at dinner."

Edie's hand stilled.

"It's that little boy, ain't it, honey?" Hazel said. "Sam McKee. I know you've been worried about him." She shook her head. "It's enough to break your heart to see how he's struggling with his mama's death."

Drawing her arm back to her side, Edie hugged herself. "Actually, it's Sam's dad, Holden. He...he asked me on a date this afternoon."

Hazel sat up straight and peered at her. "And you said?"

"I said yes, although—" Edie sighed, dropping her head back to stare up at the sky again. "—although I don't know if I should have."

Hazel pursed her lips thoughtfully. "Yes, he's got a heap of a burden on his shoulders, too. Losing his wife so young, tryin' to get over that while helpin' his son come to terms with missing his mama. It's a lot."

"I know," Edie said softly.

"I know it's just one date, but you sure you want to take that kind of burden on yourself?"

She felt herself blush and hoped the dim light hid her flushed cheeks. But her aunt must have sensed or seen her reaction, for Hazel asked quietly, "What is it, honey?"

"I want to be...oh, I want to be the *one* for a man, Aunt Hazel," she revealed on a rush. "You know, as a woman's meant to be with a man from the beginning of all time and through to the end of it, as he's meant to be for her. And because I'm the one for him, then no risk is too great to keep him from loving me with all his heart—and nothing is too great a risk for me to be with him, either." She clasped her hands around her knees and squeezed hard. "Maybe I'm being idealistic, but I don't think I'd be happy with anything less in a relationship, because—"

Because she knew what such love looked like. She'd witnessed it firsthand and knew the transforming power of it.

"You know, in Dad's last days," Edie mused aloud, "he hallucinated a lot, sometimes about when he was a boy, or about the war. But most of the time he cried for Mom, over and over, just...beseeched her to be with him, like he was calling in a promise made a long, long time ago...."

A tingling chill traveled through her in a singular moment of realization. Was *that* what frightened her about Holden? That she was on her way to falling in love with him soul-deeply, yet she knew in her heart there was no chance of him loving her the same way?

Because she'd seen his anguish when he talked of his dead wife.

"I-I guess I don't know if Holden could ever feel that way about me," she continued, almost to herself, "because if I'm not the one for him..."

Tears stung her eyes, and she pressed her forehead to her knees, trying to hold them back. If she weren't the one for him, then what cruel twist of fate would make her want him to be her one and only?

"Edie." Hazel's arms wrapped around her. "You precious, special child. I don't know what I'd do without you. But then, you were just a miracle from the day you were born, you know that, don't you? Your mama and daddy had been married twenty-two years and resigned themselves to never having children. But you obviously had other ideas, because there you came, as perfect and as wonderful as a flower opening up right before our eyes."

Edie hugged her aunt back, her heart full to bursting. "I miss them both so, Aunt Hazel."

"Oh, so do I." Her voice cracked, and Edie hugged her even more tightly. "So do I."

"I feel cheated I didn't get to spend more time with them. They'll never have the chance to know my children and watch them grow." Fiercely, Edie wiped away her tears of self-pity. "And if *I* feel that way, imagine how Holden must feel! He lost his parents when he was a boy, and now his wife. I'd find it difficult to go on, too."

Hazel sighed, chafing her niece's arm. "I don't know what to tell you, Edie. It'd be nice if we knew the whys and wherefores and whatnots of this life, but I believe that figuring that out is half the reason we're here."

Edie nodded, chin down. "That's how I feel, too. But when you come up against the loss of that one person you were meant to be with for all time, what do you do?"

"Don't know that one, either, hon," Hazel answered frankly. "Except keep connecting with people and find comfort in each other and give support. And love."

Yes, love was the bridge, between everything and everyone. She'd told Holden that. It spanned time and crossed worlds.

"But what if someone doesn't?" Edie heard her voice become agitated. She realized she had her fears, too. "What if they just continue going through life all shut up inside and never allow themselves to see the love and joy that's waiting for them here if they would just hold out their hand?"

Hazel pressed her cheek to her niece's temple. "Oh, Edie! All I can tell you is, keep on trying to be the best you know how to be. That's all you can do, honey. If that doctor is too blind or self-absorbed or grief-stricken to see what a treasure you are, then he doesn't deserve you."

Having said her piece, her aunt fell silent, and Edie reflected upon her words. They seemed as prescient as Edie's own flash of recognition. Happiness waited for everyone in this world, but it often took overcoming one's fears to find such happiness. Taking that risk required courage and faith and a certain sense of one's destiny in a defining moment in order to push past the pain and find the love waiting for you.

So *was* this her moment—with Holden? Or was she asking for something that wasn't hers to ask for?

Edie simply didn't know. All she could do was turn her eyes to the sky once more.

Chapter Seven

Sam's grin was jack-o'-lantern wide, and just as brilliant, as Hercules, controlled on a lead held by Hazel, stoically carried the boy around in a circle. Edie couldn't help thinking Sam looked as insubstantial as a cattle egret perched on the rump of a bull as he sat atop the imposing black gelding.

"Look at me, Dad! Look, Edie!" Sam crowed, excited and scared at once as he hung on to the saddle horn with both hands. "This is so cool!"

Edie noticed the horse's ears twitch at the high pitch of Sam's voice. Adding to the stir was Beauty's whining and indignant yips from the other side of the chain-link fence, where Olive had deemed it safest for the puppy to stay as long as the horse was in Hazel's yard.

"Can we go faster, Hazel?" Sam asked, slapping his feet against the horse's sides as he'd doubtless seen done in a hundred movies. Hercules' head came up with a shake.

Hazel kept a firm grip and gave a calming word to the gelding before saying to Sam, "Not today, hon. You've got a long ways to go before you're ready to take a horse by the reins."

"Really?" Sam's disappointment was palpable.

"Remember, Sam," Edie cautioned from her seat in a lawn chair under the shade of an oak tree. "Small steps at a reasonable pace—that's how you build good skills."

"I know," the boy agreed, good nature suddenly restored. He sat up straight and listened intently to Hazel's instructions to him about how to handle a horse properly.

"He sure is a different boy from six weeks ago, isn't he?" Holden said from beside her.

Edie glanced up at him as he stood with his arms crossed, his gaze following his son's every move. Today he was dressed casually in a dark green shirt open at the collar and a pair of tan chinos, both of which fit his muscular build very, very well. The color of his shirt against the background of oak leaves brought out the richness in his eyes, making their irises appear almost prismatic, a shattering of verdant hues. From this angle, the line of his strong jaw looked cleanly cut, hewn with a sharpness of purpose.

Right then, she could never see him not knowing what he wanted nor hesitating an instant to go after it.

She took a quick sip of her iced tea to ease the tightness in her throat and turned back to watching Sam, whose excitement had tempered a bit as he gave due attention to learning to steer Hercules with his knees and thighs as Hazel had told him.

He was such a serious, dear child. He'd truly stolen her heart from the beginning. Yet even before Sam, the man at her side had captured her even more completely—heart *and* soul.

"I suppose the change in Sam mostly has to do with him having some perspective from the teaching side of life's lessons," Edie responded to Holden's comment. "He tells me how you've been introducing him to the fine art of dog obedience training. Any luck getting him acquainted with dog psychology, too?"

"Dog psychology?" He raised one of those skeptical eyebrows of his. She remembered how he'd berated her about using pop psychology on his son—and giving Sam false assurances, making promises she couldn't keep.

But Edie didn't back down. "Yes. Getting Sam to think like Beauty, instead of assuming she thinks like him, as a way of training her."

"And just how does a dog think?" he asked.

"Why, with her whole heart, it's always seemed to me."

Something about her answer took him aback. *Good,* she thought, feeling a little bit more on top of the dynamics going on between them.

The illusion was brief, for a second later Holden set a hand on the back of her chair. She felt the warmth of his fingers close to her, the slightest brushing of them against her hair when she moved her head.

At that merest contact, a weakness shimmied through her, making her realize how little control she did have over the situation—and herself. *Why* did she react this way to this man? she wondered, furious with herself. She'd never experienced this kind of uncertainty before.

"It looks like Sam will be all right here with your aunt," he said. "Shall we go to dinner?"

No, she almost answered, feeling like Sam at his most rebellious. She didn't want to go, felt not at all prepared to deal with what might come.

Edie glanced up, ready to call the whole thing off, when she met Holden's eyes and was struck by the look in them. It reminded her of the first time he'd gazed intently into her eyes, so very deeply and intimately and needfully.

Like a man would gaze at a lover.

It reassured her not one bit to feel the undeniable pull of that look, for she knew that whatever moment she and Holden McKee were heading toward, there was no turning back now, no turning away.

She just never thought she would be the one reluctant to go on trust.

Dinner had not gone well.

Holden signed the credit card slip and pushed it and the pen to one side. Across the table from him, Edie sat with her eyes on her fingers as she toyed with the edge of her dinner napkin lying next to her barely touched meal.

He suppressed a sigh of frustration. He'd really hoped their time together would go better, make it easier between them. But it almost seemed they communicated best when there was some vital issue at stake. Before, that had always been Sam.

And now?

Since sharing that kiss, the critical issue, at least to Holden, had become finding that bond again. When he had, he'd simply felt he was getting close to...close to something.

Edie glanced up just then, and Holden knew she'd caught him unawares, his thoughts clear upon his face. She looked away as quickly, as if she didn't dare attend too closely.

She appeared as poised for flight as a hummingbird—Edie, the protective, loyal woman who time and again had fearlessly faced him down for the sake of his son. Right now, though, she seemed to have lost some of her strength of direction.

For some reason, such thoughts angered him.

"Is it such a trial to be with me?" Holden asked suddenly.

She looked up, surprised.

"I mean, I know I haven't always been an easy person to get along with, but I've yet to actually bite anyone, you know."

Her mouth curved into a hesitant smile. "I'm sorry, Holden. I guess I've been preoccupied." She rubbed her forehead.

"Does your head hurt?" he asked. "Sometimes tension headaches come on after the cause of the stress is alleviated, which can be confusing as to their source."

He found he wanted, if he could, to help her. But she wasn't his patient, and she seemed to recognize he'd slipped into the safe, familiar role of doctor with her even before he did, for she shook her head in answer, brown eyes knowing.

Which frustrated Holden even further. He wanted to find some way to recover that link between them again, but he knew that wouldn't be possible as long as he held back.

Well, dammit, he couldn't make himself into something that wasn't him!

The least he could do was be honest to her about it.

"Look, Edie. I'm trying here, but I don't know how to be any different than how I am. I know you'd like me to be more hopeful about the way the world works for Sam's sake, and I think I've made some progress there. But it's still difficult for me to accept that all the senseless, undeserved pain and loss that happens every single day, and not just to me or Sam personally, is meant to be. How am I supposed to believe in the future after seeing all that? It's impossible."

"I think it's in believing in the impossible that hope is born," she said, almost to herself. "And trust. Not that bad things are supposed to happen, but that what happens *does* hold meaning, even if we don't know what that meaning might be."

She'd said something like that before, and he had found it utterly naive.

"Don't you think it's just a little more complicated than that?" Holden asked with some rancor.

Her eyes flashed up at him at that, filled with her own irritation—and more. "Don't *you?* How can you know with certainty that whatever happens is senseless? Because if the bad things that happen *are* meaningless, then it follows that so must be the good things, right? How can you reduce what happiness you *have* had down to what amounts to a complete fluke?"

She was nearly distraught, he realized, and he had no idea how she'd gotten to that point. She obviously had her own doubts, almost seemed to be looking to him to discount them. But he didn't have the assurances she needed at his fingertips.

Holden sank back against the padded booth behind him. He shook his head slowly, his gaze never leaving hers. "I don't know, Edie. I suppose yes, that in a way that's how I've come to view the scheme of things, which I know is something you can't come to terms with in me."

He drew in a deep breath, made himself go on. "But then I go back to how it was the other night. I thought something had happened there, between us. Something that was real, as real as I've felt in a long time. Am I wrong?"

"No, you weren't wrong," Edie said softly. She actually flushed a delicate pink, and he felt a measure of confirmation in both his judgment and in her response. Yet there was also her response to him then, when she'd stiffened in fright.

On that thought, Holden peered at her downcast features intently and saw that she was struggling now, too—struggling to get past some misgiving to the trust she lived by so fervently.

What Holden saw was that she didn't trust *him*. At all.

She'd told him that before, but now he saw it went much deeper in her. And it hurt. Damn, but it hurt, even as he realized it was unfair of him to expect the situation to be any different. When it came right down to it, why should she trust him, for hadn't he just told her in black and white that the losses of his past prevented him from believing in his ability to promise her anything?

And she seemed to need a promise.

He didn't know what to do, could only think to utter the same request he had begun to ask of her that night on the porch.

"I know it's difficult for you," Holden said hoarsely, "but please, Edie, just don't...don't give up...."

He couldn't finish, but he guessed he'd gotten enough out, because her chin jerked up and she stared at him in wonder.

Across the table, she reached a hand out to him, and automatically he stretched his own toward her—

His cell phone rang, startling them both and wringing a stifled oath from him. Holden answered.

"Oh, Dr. McKee! Thank goodness I reached you." Hazel sounded breathless. His senses went on immediate alert. They had given her his number in case of an emergency, the possibility of which the older woman had pooh-poohed, assuring them Sam would be just fine with her and Olive to dote on him.

"It's your aunt," he said to Edie. He handed the phone to her as he leaned across the table, Edie holding the receiver so he could hear the conversation.

"It's me, Aunt Hazel. Everything okay?"

"No!" Her voice was definitely distressed. "It's...it's Sam."

Holden's stomach vaulted into his chest, lodging there and crowding his violently pounding heart.

"What's happened?" he asked into the receiver.

"I'm so sorry, Dr. McKee. I take the blame completely."

"The blame for what?" Holden said with barely contained patience.

"When Sam went outside after supper to play with Beauty, she was gone," Hazel related. "Poor little boy, he liked to've had a wall-eyed fit worrying about her."

Holden's stomach settled back into place. "Beauty just wandered off, I'm sure. She couldn't have gone far."

"That's what we thought, so we all set to looking for her in different directions, Olive and me and Sam. But you know with Olive's leg and my arthritis we don't move near as fast as a little boy does, and...oh, Dr. McKee, now we can't find Sam!"

His fear shot up again. His gaze collided with Edie's, her face inches from his, and he saw his fear reflected there, as well as something else—an acknowledgement of some point to him, it seemed.

Damn right there was a point here: he should never have set Sam loose in such unfamiliar and potentially dangerous environment.

Holden fought for control and found a slim margin of it. He couldn't think about anything else right now but locating Sam.

"He probably got involved in searching for the pup. He couldn't have gotten far," he said with as much calm as he could muster.

"But, Doctor—"

"Try not to worry, Hazel. Just keep calling for Sam. Edie and I will be there as soon as we can."

Edie nodded in vigorous agreement, her brown eyes fervent with her support. It helped, Holden realized. It helped him a lot.

He glanced out the window. "We still have a few hours of light left. Plenty of time to find him."

"But, Doctor, you don't understand!" Hazel cried. "It's not just Sam and Beauty who're missing."

His mouth went completely and utterly dry, for he knew what was coming next, even as Edie asked urgently, "Who else is gone, Aunt Hazel?"

"It's Hercules. The gate was open and his stall empty when I got there."

Edie and Holden were both out of their seats and through the door in seconds.

They arrived to find Hazel more calm, due mainly, Edie could see, to the presence of Ralph Janssen. The older couple stood on the front step, Ralph's arm around her aunt's shoulders. Olive sat in the nearby porch swing, her face careworn with worry.

Ralph gave Holden a short report on the progress of their

search so far. "We've been up and down the road in my car two miles each direction and didn't see hide nor hair of boy, pup or horse. I wouldn't let the two women here go track through the brush with the light growing dim, though they near to tore my head clean off arguin' with me over it. But the ground is rough and neither of 'em are too steady on their pins."

"You did right, Mr. Janssen," Holden agreed, although Edie could see he was impatient to be away.

"Now that Holden and I are here," she spoke up, "how about we grab some flashlights and get started down toward the creek."

She wouldn't let herself begin to dwell on what might happen to a boy or a puppy or a horse coming upon a steep-banked stream in the failing light. But she could see Holden's thoughts had already gone there.

Within minutes the three of them were spread out along a line a hundred yards wide as they tramped through the thick grass. Edie called Sam's name over and over, and could hear Ralph and Holden doing the same, Holden's voice charged with a jagged edge of fear. She tried to send out her support to him in her thoughts but felt her efforts fell far short of the mark, for mingled with her own fear was her sense of responsibility for this new crisis concerning Sam.

Was *this* what the visions had forewarned her of, and she'd let her preoccupation with Holden blind her to the warning signs of it happening? She didn't think she would forgive herself if some harm befell Sam. She had a feeling that neither would Holden forgive himself—or her.

With effort, Edie got a grip on herself. She couldn't have known; she had no special foresight. And she couldn't live her life in trepidation of what might happen, couldn't let Sam live his that way, not when the boy was slowly learning to be happy again.

But if Holden chose to live his life that way, *was* there anything she could do about it?

They found Hercules first, in the patch of grass where he and Fancy had been the day Sam had first come to visit. Holden's grim gaze met hers across the small clearing. The gelding was grazing calmly enough, but that didn't mean he might not have been spooked recently by the high-pitched sound of a little boy's voice or the frenzied barking of an excited pup.

"Let's start searching the ground in a circle from around the horse," Holden said without inflection as Ralph hobbled the horse as a precaution. Edie knew Holden was keeping close check on his emotions right now, as was she. It was the only way to keep fear from taking over.

Edie slapped at a mosquito as she swept her flashlight in an arc back in forth in front of her. There was still light, but she was taking no chances as she alternately prayed they'd find Sam here—and that they would not find him, either lying unconscious in the grass or with a puppy who'd gotten too close.

Even with the flashlight, though, Edie found it difficult to see where to place her steps in the thick underbrush. She'd just come around the trunk of a large tree, gaze trained ahead of her, when she walked right into the creek.

Its depth was no more than a foot, yet Edie found herself reacting as if she'd gone in over her head as she gave a gasp of sheer terror. She knew she'd always been uncomfortable around water, but now she realized just how deep-seated her fear of it was.

Because the danger rose up around her in a choking fog.

In absolute panic, she jumped back, the flashlight flying from her hand. The back of her head thunked up against something hanging from the limb of the tree. Her scalp tingled.

Edie screamed and whirled, ready to defend her life. Her breath caught—then rushed out in relief.

Sam sat on a low branch of the tree, his sneakered feet dangling, his expression a mirror image of his father's dark one. He stared at her rebelliously. It was clear to her the boy wouldn't have said a word, would have let her walk right past him, had she not stumbled into the creek and then upon him.

Her fear converted to exasperation with Sam in an instant. "Sam McKee, what on earth did you think you were doing with that horse? You *promised* me you'd be careful!"

She realized within a split second her mistake, for Sam didn't say a word in response as his chin tucked lower and a charged stillness radiated from him.

"All right," she said more moderately, gesturing with her hand. "Come on down and let's talk."

For a moment he didn't move, and she thought she'd have a tussle on her hands, but then the boy scooted over to the trunk of the tree and deftly hoisted himself to the ground. Once there, though, he resumed his tense, unreachable stance.

She cupped her hands around her mouth and gave a call to Holden and Ralph. Then she set her fists on her hips and regarded Sam. She wanted to pull him to her in a hug of reassurance but knew any physical demonstration would most definitely be rejected by the boy right now. Instead, Edie crouched in front of him, looking him in the eye.

"Sam. I didn't mean to scold you when I haven't even given you a chance to explain what happened. But you can understand, can't you, how much I feared for you when Hazel told us you and Beauty were missing? When we found out Hercules was gone, too…"

She swallowed hard, even now the frightful images of what might have occurred vivid in her mind. She still could have shaken him for being so foolhardy, and she understood better than ever Holden's anger—not so much at Sam, but at how little control one had in this world, how hard it was to open your heart and trust when you could lose someone in the blink of an eye, with no warning…and no apparent reason.

"I was scared for you, Sam," she said, reaching out to

touch him, needing to, with the brush of her fingers through his hair. "Both your father and I were."

He didn't shun her touch, but neither did he respond to it as he looked at her watchfully.

There was a crashing through the neighboring underbrush, and then Holden appeared, his face a study in sheer dreadedness of what he would find.

His expression cleared as soon as he spied his son, safe and sound. "Sam! Thank God."

Though Sam was apparently oblivious to his father's spontaneous invocation, Holden held out his arms as he took two quick steps toward his son, who didn't look up at his father's arrival or acknowledge him in any way.

Holden stopped. Edie saw his jaw go rigid. He dropped his arms.

She rose, moving almost involuntarily closer to Sam. Holden marked that shift in position. His jaw veritably bulged.

"What happened?" he asked. It was unclear whether he addressed her or Sam, so Edie answered.

"I don't know exactly. I only found him just now."

Holden turned to his son. "What happened, Sam? I know Beauty ran away, but how did Hazel's horse get out of his stall?"

Sam lowered his eyebrows even further, until they nearly touched in the middle, and his mouth remained pinched shut.

"Did you let Hercules out of his stall, Sam?" Edie asked gently.

Another hesitation, then he nodded curtly. "I was gonna ride him only he ran away."

"Good Lord, you could have been trampled or worse!" Holden gave a heavy sigh. "Sam, why on earth would you do such a thing?"

Sam stood as still as stone. No reaction at all, although the boy's face grew even darker with an emotion Edie recognized as anger. Still he held it all in.

She caught Holden's eye. "Perhaps it would be better if we pursued this later," she murmured. "So everyone would have time to regain their perspective."

He stared at her, slowly shaking his head. "No. This isn't going to get turned into some kind of boys-will-be-boys adventure again. Sam needs to know in no uncertain terms that what he did was dangerous and wrong."

He squatted in front of his son, taking him by the upper arms not ungently. "Why did you do it, Sam? Were you thinking riding Hercules would make it easier to find Beauty?"

At the mention of the puppy's name, the child wrenched himself free of his father's grip. "No!"

"Then why, son?"

"I just...I just...I wanted to feel what it was like to fly!" he finally burst out, his mouth twisting in anguish. "I know you tol' me I'd work up to it, but I wanted to do it now, that's all, even if it was a dumb idea."

"Oh, Sam," Edie murmured, slipping her arm around his shoulder. But he shook it off furiously and stood facing both her and Holden with his fists clenched at his sides, gray eyes defiant and fierce.

Now Holden grew very still, his gaze riveted on his son. His voice fell softly in the night air as he asked, "Why has it been so important for you to fly, Sam?"

"Because I wanted to see if I could touch heaven!" Sam cried, as if making a shameful confession. "I wanted to see if...if I could touch Mom."

He tipped his head back and looked up at the dusky sky, dry-eyed and searching, and Edie's heart cracked in two for him, for his heartache was so deep and solitary.

Her gaze flew to Holden, who had made not a move.

"I see you found Sam" came Ralph's voice in the distance. "And here's the little girl."

Edie turned to see the older man climbing the slope, holding a docile puppy in his arms. "Found her all tangled up in a blackberry thicket, poor thing. She was sure one sceered pup."

Beauty whined faintly as Ralph drew closer, and she began to wriggle impatiently, becoming quite a handful to hang on to. Ralph apparently decided she'd learned her lesson and stooped to set her on the ground. As soon as her paws touched it, she came galloping the rest of the way toward them, heading straight for Sam. With a yip of thankfulness, she jumped up on him, her tongue flicking out to lick him as she begged for his forgiving caress.

But Sam wasn't about to give any such assurance. Instead, he stuffed his hands into the pockets of his shorts and turned away—looking for all the world as if the puppy didn't exist to him.

Gazing after him quizzically, Beauty sank down on her haunches, the wag in her snippet tail slowing to nothing.

The scene made by boy and pup just about brought Edie to tears, for it confirmed exactly what she had so feared moments ago as she'd searched for him, her heart in her throat. It was not Sam's physical well-being that was so in peril at this moment in time, but his emotional well-being—the part of him that still hoped, still trusted, still allowed himself to love.

And still, Holden did not stir to comfort his son.

Go to him! she relayed to him with all her being. *Say something. Reach out and touch him, and refuse to be pushed away. Anything! Just don't let him feel so alone right now—or so bad for wanting the impossible. Because if you don't do something, you'll lose him, this time for good.*

But the man across from her was apparently on a completely different wavelength, one she didn't and would never understand. She wasn't the kind of person who could close herself off to protect herself from giving all the love she could give to another for fear of how much it would hurt to lose them.

She couldn't be that way, and she couldn't fall in love with someone who was.

Yet she found herself even more moved as she beheld Holden standing motionless, as if impaled through the heart by the picture those two lost little souls made. His face was ravaged by the emotions he, too, kept locked inside.

He, too, stood alone and aching, caught in a web of ill-fated circumstances spun long ago.

She couldn't not do it. She could not prevent herself from reaching out to him right now, no matter what had or might occur, if there was the glimmer of a hope of pulling him out of the cave he'd retreated into, to inspire in him a response, as he had started to do in the restaurant when he'd almost begged her not to give up in that way so like the boy in her vision.

Edie slipped up beside him. She wanted to take his hand, but both were firmly buried in his pockets. She settled for resting her hand on his shoulder with a squeeze and hoped it helped.

He very nearly flinched at that contact before moving away.

The rejection hurt her to her core, but the emptiness she felt was what resounded to her soul.

"I'll just go fetch Hercules," Ralph said quietly.

"Th-thanks, Ralph," Edie said, watching him disappear into the falling twilight before bending and scooping into her arms the one being who'd accept her comfort right now. Shivering, Beauty gave a little whimper and snuggled against Edie's chest, inserting her cold, wet nose into the crook of her neck.

It helped, Edie found, on both sides.

They walked single file back to the house, silent as monks on their way to vespers. Hazel and Olive waited tensely on the porch and met the group as the three of them drew within the circle of the porch light.

"Everyone's been found and is safe," Edie said, answering their unasked question. "Ralph's coming with Hercules."

"Thank goodness!" Hazel said fervently, palm flattened to

her chest. She met Holden at the bottom of the steps. "I can't tell you, Doctor, how sorry I am this happened."

"Please, Hazel, it's not your fault." He looked down at his son, who stood at his side. "Sam, I think you owe the ladies an apology for letting Hercules out of his stall, then taking off into the woods and causing them so much worry."

To his credit, Sam roused himself from his detached state and looked both women in the eye, saying, "I'm sorry. I shouldna gone near Hercules by myself, like you tol' me."

Hazel skimmed her hand over the boy's dark head. "Oh, hon, we were just scared something might have happened to you."

As when Edie had voiced such fear to him, Sam gazed at Hazel fixedly, although his expression remained inscrutably blank.

Without looking at his father, he said, "Can we go home now, Dad?"

"Sure." He seemed to rouse himself, too, enough to ask in a muted voice, "Would you like to bring Beauty with us? I'm sure her spending one night at the town house would be allowed."

Sam gave a shrug of utter indifference. "I don't care."

Edie could see he did not. Not at all. Experiencing the abandonment by his pup, even temporarily, had been the last nail in the coffin of this child's ability to hope.

"We should be going," Holden answered without emotion.

Good-nights echoed in the damp evening air before Holden and Sam started for their car.

"Won't you say good-night to Beauty, Sam?" Edie asked in a strangled voice, finding it impossible not to try, one last time, to keep this boy from losing all will to keep seeking his happiness. To keep him from believing it wasn't worth the pain to try.

He walked right past her.

Heartsick, she turned desperately to his father. "Please,

Holden. Don't let him retreat all the way into his shell. This is a crucial moment for him—and you. He's yearning toward something and I'm afraid of what will happen to him if he isn't able to find it and take hold."

"Thank you for your concern, Edie," he answered. "I'll handle it."

But she could see clearly he was at a loss as to how to do that.

"At least take Beauty with you so he has the chance to make up with her," she suggested, stroking the dog's silky ears.

"No." No indecision there. "I think the pup's done enough damage for tonight." He started after Sam.

Edie's hand shot out of its own volition, grabbing his forearm. "Don't let this matter slide, Holden. Please. Keep reaching out to him—for Sam's sake."

For the first time since they'd left the clearing, Holden met her eyes. *Speaking of retreating into shells,* Edie thought, although she saw, at the back of his somber gaze, that ember of hope or need to connect that he'd begged her not to let die.

Then he turned and was gone.

Edie stood staring after him, her arms wrapped around her waist, torn in two by indecision. She felt a comforting arm go around her.

"Oh, Aunt Hazel, what's going to happen to them?" she choked.

"I don't know. Maybe it's not up to you or me."

"But I feel so...so useless just standing here while they're suffering so!"

"You can't be another's savior, hon," Hazel said. "It's like you said. Whatever happiness and love those two are going to find, they've both got to reach out for it. And they'll either find it or they won't."

Edie knew the truth in her aunt's words. Knew it was the

way things worked in this life. And that there was meaning in both the good and the bad of it.

Don't give up on me, Holden had implored her, both in her visions and for real. There was meaning in that, too, although she still didn't know what it was.

Hitching the puppy under one arm, Edie took off for her car.

Chapter Eight

Edie pulled into the parking lot of the town-house complex where Holden and Sam lived. To her relief, she'd caught up with them just before they'd gotten on the freeway and had been able to follow them here.

She watched as father and son walked to the door of one of the units and went inside. She glanced at Beauty, who lay curled up on the front passenger seat and looked the epitome of dog-tired after all her excitement today. As long as the puppy wasn't restless, Edie decided to leave her in the car for now. She could fetch her once the situation had been settled. Hopefully, it would be.

She cracked the windows before leaving the car and stealing up to the door she'd seen Holden and Sam go through. Edie knocked softly.

Holden answered the door. His bearing went on full alert at the sight of her.

"I had to come," Edie said quickly. "I had to. I brought Beauty," she added with defiance. "She's out in the car."

He didn't invite her in, but rather left her standing at the open front door while he walked back into the house. With a proprietary air she didn't entirely embrace, Edie entered the small foyer and closed the door behind her as she had a quick look around.

The town house was just how Sam described it: the rooms, while filled with furniture and decorated pleasantly, were virtually devoid of any enlivening or personal features. In her estimation, the whole place cried out for signs of life—the odd family photo or first-grade art project, a comfortable if frumpy recliner. Even a pair of beat-up sneakers set at the foot of the steps to be taken up the next time someone went upstairs would have been welcomed.

Yes, the stairs—where Sam had taken his leap of faith.

On the upper floor, she peeked into the first bedroom along the hallway and saw the boy where he sat alone on the edge of his bed, facing away from the door in the darkened room, the only illumination coming from the window.

He looked like the incarnation of absolute hopelessness.

"Sam?" she said softly. "How're you doing, champ?"

He revealed no sign of having heard her, and her heart grew heavy all over again. Any reaction would have been better than none, but as he'd said, he just didn't care.

Her impatience with Holden building, Edie set off in search of him.

She found him in an upstairs bathroom rummaging through the medicine cabinet. Crossing her arms, Edie leaned against the doorjamb.

"I was just getting some calamine lotion," Holden explained shortly. "Sam got a couple of nasty mosquito bites out there tonight."

He seemed not at all happy to see her. Well, that was just too darn bad, Edie thought.

He found the bottle he was looking for and started for the doorway, which she blocked. She raised one eyebrow—his old trick.

"Look," he said, with a bit of his own impatience, "I know tending to Sam's physical hurts is not what you think he needs from me right now, but I *am* a doctor and that's the best I can do at the moment!"

Holden pushed past her, striding down the hallway to Sam's room, but once there he stopped outside, and Edie knew he looked at the same desolate sight she just had. He turned, saw her standing there.

Shaking his head, he closed his eyes and sank back against the wall. "Oh, *Edie.*"

She swept past him to shut Sam's door before facing him.

He still shook his head, tipped back against the wall behind him. "I never should have let him get up on that horse. Or have that puppy."

"Why?"

"I knew the moment would come when she'd break his heart." His Adam's apple bobbed as he swallowed. "He's shut her out, don't you see, out of fear of being abandoned again, as he believes he was by...by his mother."

He opened his eyes and looked down at her, bleakness written into every line of his features. "That's why he decided he had to try to fly right then. So he could...so he could touch Heaven. Touch her. But he can't. He can't ever touch her again. She's gone."

The anguish in his voice tore her to pieces. Oh, to have been loved like that! The yearning nearly brought her to tears.

Stalwartly, Edie pushed such thoughts back into their corner. Right now, she must concentrate on helping the two who remained behind.

"But you and Sam have each other, Holden," she said urgently. "That's what counts. Comforting each other, reaching out to each other. A simple touch is all it takes. Really."

He seemed not to hear her, seemed immersed in his own private hell of isolation and hopelessness.

She couldn't let him remain there.

Edie lifted her hand, ready to set it upon his shoulder as before, and paused. *That's not what I need from you,* he'd told her once.

She knew what he did need from her. He'd shown her. But could she give it without losing a piece of herself in the process?

Her heart thudding, Edie switched the direction of her gesture—and laid her palm against Holden's cheek in a lover's caress.

For a moment all she could do was feel. The sandpapery surface was so familiar to her, although she'd only touched him once this way, and she couldn't resist grazing the side of her thumb against that firm, rough expanse of skin.

How she wanted him! Even knowing his heart was another's didn't change that.

His lashes flickered as his gaze homed in on her eyes, then dropped to her mouth.

"Go to him, Holden," she whispered while she had this connection, was able to speak to his heart and know he heard. "Talk to him. Don't let him push you away. Help him to make sense of what's happened. Help yourself, too."

His jaw muscle pulsed under her palm. "I...I don't know what to say to him. Good Lord, Edie, how can I teach him how to hope when I don't believe in hope myself?"

"Just...try. Won't you try?"

His eyes grew remote. She was losing him. "There's nothing I can say to him that would make sense to either one of us, believe me."

Yes, she understood the losses he'd endured, the pain and fear and heart-wrenching hurt he'd gone through losing his wife, and she ached for him having to live through that.

But now their son was in turmoil, and this man had the power if not the God-given obligation to rise to the occasion, to set aside past doubts, no matter how great or how deeply imbedded, and do what was right for his son.

Edie dropped her hand and stepped right up to Holden, got right in his face.

"That does it," she said. "I don't care what it takes, Holden McKee. You get past your anger or your cynicism or your fear or *whatever* it is that holds you back and you go to your son! You'll think of something to say, and even if you don't, right now your silent comfort and understanding is worth more than a thousand words of wisdom to that boy."

She pointed at Sam's door. "You might never get another chance, Holden. Let it go by and you'll lose Sam, maybe not in the way your wife or your parents or even your dog was taken from you, but he'll be lost to you, j-just the same."

She choked on the last words, so afraid Holden himself was lost to her. But she'd had to try, just one more time.

He stared at her, eyes of gray-green turning as cold as marble. Had she pushed too far this time? But what else was she to have done? There was so much at stake, and not just for Sam.

The moment seemed to hang, a second's worth of delay, like a ripple in time.

Holden nodded once. Turned. And walked away.

Edie could only stare after him in disbelief, sick to her stomach. And disappointed to her very soul.

When Holden came back down the hallway, he saw clearly on Edie's face that she hadn't expected him to return. His fingers clenched the soft object in his hand.

He didn't know how he was going to do this, was petrified of failing, for he feared not only never having another chance to bring his son back from the depths of a despair he was far too well-acquainted with, but that he would blow this chance at redemption.

Then both their souls would be lost.

He stopped in front of the door to Sam's room. Apparently

understanding his intent, Edie began to slip away, to give them privacy, he was sure. His hand shot out and grabbed hers.

"Don't go, please," he whispered. He didn't know why, but her silent support was about all that was going to get him through this. He rubbed his thumb over her knuckles. "Just...stay."

Head down, the curtain of her hair shielding her face, she nodded once. "All right. But only so long as I feel my presence isn't intruding."

With a deep breath, Holden let go of her hand and took the knob, opening the door to Sam's room. Inside, his son still sat on the edge of his bed, tucked into himself, chin touching his chest, shoulders crumpled inward. *Abandonment* was written in every line of his small body.

In that instant, Holden saw himself as he had never perceived his own being. Saw from an outside perspective the boy who, ripe with the smell of river water and soaked to the skin, had shivered under a blanket pulled around his shoulders by his uncle in a vain attempt to provide comfort. Yet the circumstances had been such that such comfort could do little good.

How could it, when he had lost everything?

The remembered pain came stampeding over him, a thousand sharp hooves gouging into tender skin, each a biting reminder of what he'd said goodbye to that day, his innocence about life not among the least of it.

He made an involuntary sound halfway between a groan and a gasp. Sam turned, his little boy face haggard, hopeless. Then he spied what his father held in one hand.

"It's Bear!" he cried.

Holden found his legs, came around to the side of the bed where Sam sat and handed him the bedraggled terry-cloth bear. His son took it almost reverently.

Sam looked up at him as if disbelieving his own eyes, then clasped the bear to his chest.

"I thought he was gone forever," he breathed. "You saved him?"

Holden crouched in front of the boy. "I spotted him in the Goodwill box in the laundry room a few months ago. I took him out and put him away. I thought you might want him some day when...some day."

"I din't think I would," Sam admitted. He shot Holden a suspicious glance. "How did *you* know, though?"

Holden clasped his hands between his thighs. "I had a box of belongings when I was a boy. It was like...like a treasure box, with its own secret hiding place and everything."

"What was in it?" Sam asked. Holden deemed his curiosity a good sign.

"Oh, bits and pieces of things you wouldn't even think important." He swallowed, then made himself go on, "Mostly mementos of my mother and father. And my dog. Remember I told you a little about her when you first got Beauty?"

Sam concentrated inordinately on trying to push one of the bear's button eyes, which was hanging by a thread, back into its socket.

"Anyway," Holden continued, "I lost that box, but I think about it sometimes and wish I had it, or even just one thing out of it to remember them by."

"But it hurts to remember." Sam's voice was soft.

Holden wanted to reach out to his son, connect with him, but the building ache in his chest kept him from doing so. He had to maintain control of it. Yet he was deathly afraid he wouldn't be able to.

"Yes, it hurts," he said. "But it can help to remember, too, I've discovered. I hope you'll feel that way, too, some day."

Just a hint of finality had somehow crept into that last statement, Holden realized, as if the subject had reached its end.

Yet Sam's eyebrows puckered in question. "You mean Bear might help me to remember Mom?"

A certain panic rose in Holden, which he concentrated on

pushing down so he could answer his son. "Yes, just like Beauty can help you to deal with the hurt of losing her, too."

He nodded toward the doorway, where Edie stood, her face in shadows. "Edie brought Beauty with her, you know. She's outside in the car."

Sam ducked his head, now clearly disturbed by the mention of the puppy.

With his eyes, Holden implored Edie for her help. She moved not a muscle, yet he felt her support and encouragement roll over him in a wave of emotion. He didn't think he could have gone on without it.

"Look, son." He tilted his head, trying to meet Sam's gaze. "Beauty is your responsibility now, whether you feel like taking care of her or not. You chose to make her a part of your life, not her. You owe her the best of your love and care and protection."

Sam's face took on that closed aspect he'd worn just after Edie had found him this evening. It was as if the boy physically shut himself off from the outside world. Or was holding the pain all inside. How well Holden knew the feeling!

How was he to reach his son?

Then, just as it had earlier, Sam's quandary burst out of him. "But Beauty ran away! She left *me!*"

His mouth worked as he tried not to cry. Bear was getting the life squeezed out of him.

Holden set one hand on the bed next to his son. "Beauty didn't leave you on purpose. She's just a puppy, Sam. She probably sniffed some curious new smell and it took her away from the house and she got lost before she even knew it. Likely, it was her trying to find you that got her even more lost, you know?"

Sam shook his head furiously. Obviously, he didn't know.

"You're her whole world, son." Holden heard his voice grow rough. "You can't let her down."

"But what if I make a mistake?" Sam asked, his own voice

filled with an anguish he couldn't contain any longer. "What if somethin' happens to me and I can't be there for her?"

"Nothing's going to happen to you, Sam," Holden vowed. God help him, he couldn't let the moment go by without giving his son such an assurance.

Yet Sam, his father's son, was not so easily assured. "No, but what if it did?" he insisted. "Edie was scared something had, you know. So was Hazel and Olive. They thought I got hurt. What if *I* die, Dad? What'll happen to Beauty?" He stared at Holden with large, frightened eyes. "What'll happen to *you?* You'll be all alone!"

That was it. Holden couldn't respond for a long, long moment, as memories rose up around him like ghosts from a child's worst nightmare.

Rain pouring down. A river raging out of control. Death stalking them both, having already taken his dear mother. Only one would live. And one would be left behind. To do what?

"You can't hold back from loving someone out of fearing either one of you will be taken away," Holden choked out, feeling such a platitude inadequate in the extreme.

"But it hurts!" Sam cried. "It hurts to think about Mom. Oh, why did she have to die?"

The entreaty to understand came up from the bottom of the boy's being, gut-wrenching and hoarse.

"I don't know, son. I truly don't know." Holden felt sick in spirit that he had no answer for his son, for it was the same question that barraged his mind ten times a day. Why did anything happen on this earth?

But he must say something! Now, above any other time in his life, he must come through for Sam.

Tell me, he beseeched his consciousness, the heart of him, his very soul. *Tell me what to say to him. Please, give me the words. Please.*

Then, without him fully comprehending how it happened, the words were there.

"Don't you think there could still be a reason your mother died, Sam, even if you and I don't know what that is?" Holden asked. "I mean, we're surrounded by a whole world of things no one couldn't begin to say how they worked. Even if we do know, scientifically, how a flower knows to bloom, how the earth turns around the sun, how a baby can grow from just a tiny speck, it's still a mystery how they all seem to happen. What I mean is, even if you didn't understand a thing about how the world operates, the fact is it still does. So couldn't it be possible that, even if you or I might not understand why something happens, there's still a reason it does. And that there's some meaning in what happens."

"But what do you do if you don't *know?*" Sam whispered, the significance of the moment apparently affecting him, too.

"You just have to...trust," he said. He knew he was spouting Edie's philosophy right now, one he'd denounced from the beginning. But right now it made sense—for Sam. "Keep believing in doing impossible things like flying and touching heaven. Because when you can begin to believe in the impossible, that's when hope is born."

Still, Sam had yet to be convinced, for the boy's face screwed up in abrupt anger. "But *you* don't! You don't believe. You don't talk about Mom. You don't want to remember her. It's like you never cared!"

Ah, now they were getting to the heart of the matter, Holden thought.

"I did," he said huskily. He lifted his hand and ran his fingers through his son's dark hair. His son. "I do. But I lost my dad when I was just about the age you are now. Then I lost my mom, not long after. When I lost your mother, it brought up a whole lot of those memories, and they hurt. It was...hard to deal with those feelings. But that doesn't mean

I didn't love her. In fact, I can't imagine what my life would have been like not to have loved her."

He lifted Sam's chin, looking him straight in the eye. "Because without that love, Sam, I'd never have been given the chance to love you."

He watched his son peer at him, gray eyes direct and piercing and looking right into his heart—looking for the truth. Holden knew that if Sam didn't find it there, all would be lost forever. The boy had to know that his father believed what he was saying, or Sam could not believe.

His gut twisted. He *had* loved Rose, very much. And given the chance, maybe he would have eventually been able to give her the kind of love she deserved that held nothing back, nothing in reserve to stave off the pain in case that love should be taken away.

But he was not to be given that chance. That hurt, too, more than he could say. Yet was that enough reason to hold himself back from the one he'd been given right now?

Holden met his son's gaze without faltering.

After a moment, Sam set Bear aside and slid off the bed to go to his dresser in the corner. He knelt and opened the bottom drawer, pawed through stacks of sweatshirts and jeans, and finally found what he was after. He pulled it out and sat on his heels, looking at it. He rose and turned, and took it to his father.

Holden drew the boy between his knees, and they both studied the photo of a woman with soft brown hair and gentle blue eyes.

"She was pretty, wasn't she?" Holden said quietly. Sam nodded, the back of his head bumping Holden's chin. "You've got her nose, you know."

"I do?" The boy reached up and touched that part of his face.

"Mm-hmm. You also inherited your mother's love of the outdoors. Her seriousness and compassion, too."

"What's that, compassion?"

"It's being able to feel deeply for others' concerns." He put an arm around the boy's waist and snuggled him closer, wondering at how long it had been since he'd sat this way with his own son. "I think...it's right that you grieve her. That you want to keep her alive in your heart so much you try to touch her. And she's reaching out to you, too. Right now. She knows you miss her, Sam. She didn't want to go, either. But she'd want you to go on and try to be happy—would want that for both of us."

Sam sniffed. He turned frantic eyes up toward his father. Holden didn't look away, didn't try to blink back the moisture forming under his lids.

And hope finally came in the shape of a single tear. And then another, and another. One by one Sam's tears fell, spilling down cheeks and nose and mouth and chin. His relief like an ocean, Holden rocked his son in his arms, and the tears fell harder as Sam's small body was racked by sobs that came in great gusts of emotion, so long had it been checked.

"That's it. Let it out, son," Holden whispered, cheek pressed to his boy's head. "We've both been holding back much too long."

In the background, he heard the door close and footsteps retreating down the hall.

It took a while, but at last Sam quieted. And still Holden held him. He felt shaky inside, like he'd run a marathon. Sam, too, seemed rag-doll dragged out, and he was even dozing against his father's chest.

Yet he stirred himself enough to say, "I think...I think I'd like to see Beauty now. She's prob'ly still scared, and I need to tell her it's all right."

Holden thought he'd burst with pride. "That's the right thing to do, son."

"Yeah, it is," the boy said with a tinge of amazement. "I'm

not going to quit loving her, either, out of being scared. I don't want her thinkin' she can't count on me, y'know?"

"I know." Holden smiled. "And that's just as it should be, Sam."

Holden gave his son a parting squeeze and let him go. The boy scooted around the edge of the bed and hauled open the door before dashing through it, all hopeful expectation now that the heartache had been well and truly purged.

"And that's just as it should be," Holden repeated softly.

From the confines of the tiny enclosed patio at the back of Holden's town house, Edie peered up at the sky. The stars were there somewhere, she was sure, but with all the ambient light from the surrounding businesses and neighborhoods, only the brightest held any chance of shining through.

The patio door slid open behind her.

"Did you get Beauty set up in Sam's room?" she asked, not turning. A slight breeze raised goose bumps on her arms, and she chafed them nervously.

"Yes, but only after she piddled on the carpet in one corner, as well as chewed the laces up on one of his tennis shoes when I'd left for a few minutes to get something to clean the puddle up with and Sam had gone to brush his teeth. I'm just going to go on down to the leasing office tomorrow and tell them I've got a puppy here for a few weeks and sign away my security deposit."

Edie had to laugh. "It might be a good idea to set a wake-up call for the middle of the night so one of you can take her out for a potty break. Otherwise you might have another unpleasant surprise."

"Good idea. I'll put an alarm clock in Sam's room for him to get up." There was a pause. "Beauty is his dog. His responsibility. He may as well find out right away what that fully means."

"You're not afraid any longer he'll get too attached to her

and get his heart broken?" Edie asked gently, already knowing the answer but wanting to hear Holden say it.

"No. I'm not afraid of that any longer." His voice was hushed. "I have you to thank for getting me to that point of being able to reach him."

"I refuse to take any credit. You were wonderful with him." She had to tell him. "Holden, I know how hard that was for you to think about those times in your past, to think about your wife, but you found inside you what was needed and shared it with Sam. And I'm...I'm so very glad for you both."

She *was* glad, even if her gladness held a bittersweetness she was finding hard to reconcile in her heart. She had wanted for weeks for both Holden and Sam to take that turn in their mourning and grief to where they started to look forward again, and from what she had heard pass between them, they had. It heartened her no end. But she was ashamed of her feelings of wanting a love such as Holden had clearly had for his dead wife, for she'd also heard the heartache in his voice that seemed wrenched from his vitals when he talked about her.

And Edie wanted that sort of love—with *him*. But it seemed impossible.

She heard him move behind her, heard the creak of an aluminum lawn chair as he sat in it. From a distance came the sound of heavy traffic, even at this hour of the evening.

"You know, I hadn't thought about my boyhood years in Texas for a long time," he said at last. "And then—it was almost eerie how it happened just at this point in time—I got a call a few days ago from Tim Appleby, a guy I knew when we were both kids in East Texas. Seems his mother had to come over to Grace Hospital for some tests and saw or heard my name while she was a patient. Mrs. Appleby mentioned it to her son, who decided to look me up and see if I was the same Holden McKee from twenty-odd years ago."

The chair squeaked again as he shifted in it. "Tim was one of the kids my father's efforts saved during that flu epidemic."

"I can see why he wanted to find out if you were the boy he once knew, and wanted to renew the connection," Edie said simply.

"Yes," Holden mused, his voice in her ear, "that...need to connect. Like how it is between us."

With a start, Edie realized he had risen and now stood close behind her. Her heart started pounding so hard it felt bruised.

"I need it, Edie," he continued, his voice at a pitch that evoked images of velvet and silk. "This connection. I don't understand it. When I'm away from you and try remembering how it felt, it almost seems like I must have been imagining its power, and nothing could be that strong. Then all I have to do is feel your touch, or touch you, and it's as powerful and real as anything I've ever experienced in my whole life."

Despite herself, hope started up in her like a flock of doves set loose in the sky.

"What do you mean?" Edie asked, still not daring to turn and look at him for fear he'd see such a desperate yearning in her eyes.

"I don't know. Part of it, I think, is how you seem to make me feel more grounded. It has such an effect on me, in a lot of ways, like I'm more in tune with things. With Sam. With my patients, even."

He gave a low chuckle. "Listen to me. I sound like you, 'picking up on things.'"

That tender kind of laugh, like one between lovers—it sent a tingling crackling up her spine to her scalp. Edie quickly snuffed it out, apprehensive of getting too used to enjoying it.

"You would have found the strength to do the right thing eventually, for both you and Sam," she said. "And you'll continue to, with or without me."

"Yes, well, that remains to be seen," Holden returned cryptically. Then his hands stole up her arms with a feather touch that nearly made her knees give out. "Right now, though, I'm wondering about you. What you feel."

Oh please, her heart cried out, *I can't take this, not if it's not real and lasting.*

But if his revelation about his late wife wanting both Sam and him to go on and be happy wasn't about believing in the future again, even in the impossible, then what was? And Edie wanted to believe, too, so very badly.

Yet she had to know for sure. Whatever the outcome, it would be better to know the truth.

"Sam's mother," she said. "You l-loved her very much, didn't you?"

He went still. "Yes. Yes, I did."

Oh, she thought she would die!

Then he went on in a low tone, "But I have to be honest with you, Edie. With myself. I could have loved Rose more."

Her heart stopped completely. "I don't understand," Edie said in utter confusion.

He dropped his hands, his voice seeming to take on his old detachment as he answered, "I always held back some part of myself from her, out of fear, I think. I was afraid to love and lose her. Except the fact is, in the end, I lost her, anyway. I see now that the solution was not to love her less than I could have, but more."

He paused, drawing a breath before going on. "And it's a failure I'll live with for the rest of my life."

Edie couldn't speak for several moments, her thoughts in turmoil. She'd been so afraid to learn from Holden how he could never love another woman as he loved his dead wife that Edie could barely take in his admission that he hadn't. So why didn't she consider this hopeful news?

Not knowing how else to react, Edie finally said, "I'm sorry, Holden."

"Sorry? It's not your fault."

It was what he'd said before, when she'd expressed sympathy for his and Sam's loss. It was his way of detaching himself from emotions that ran too deeply.

"I know that," she answered a bit defensively, hugging herself. "I only meant I'd have liked for there to have been more. For your wife. For *you*, I mean. F-for it to have been different for you! But you can't go back and rewrite the past. None of us can."

"No, we can't." Oh, he'd definitely distanced himself. She heard it in every chilly word. "Much as we might want to."

And yet some longing inside of her wanted for the past to have been different. "It's just that...that..."

It was just that nagging apprehension that hovered at the back of her consciousness—was it that still unidentifiable sense of danger she'd experienced in her visions? Did she want to know?

"It's just what, Edie? That's what I'm wondering. You've never held back before about what you thought or felt or wanted—you've always known what it was and reached out for it with both hands." Warmth emanated from him as he moved closer, his chest against her back. "Where's that sureness of direction now that's so much a part of you?"

She shook her head in confusion. She could have cried. In fact, the tears swelled in her eyes. "I don't know!"

He turned her toward him then, his hands gripping her upper arms. And unquestionably some force surged through her at his touch. "What don't you know? Or let me guess. Granted I'm not too great at this touchy-feely stuff, but am I way out in left field here, thinking you feel the same kind of power I feel when we touch? Or is it just me?"

"Yes!" she burst out. "It's you!"

Sparks shot from his eyes, but even through a haze of emotion she knew he wasn't angry with her. He made an inarticulate sound, then somehow she was locked in his arms as he bent his head to take her lips as if it were his birthright.

Heaven help her, Edie rose up to meet him with every bit

of her soul, fingers clenching his shirtfront, her chin straining upward to make his mouth one with hers.

Like before, there was nothing delicate in his kiss. The emotion was too great, the need too critical, as if their lives depended upon it.

He lifted his chin barely a fraction of an inch to mutter huskily, "So it's just me, is it?"

"Yes," Edie whispered. "It *is* you, Holden."

He swore. "How can you say that?" he demanded, his expression pure frustration.

She looked at him boldly, and for the moment she was unafraid. Because sometimes the heart will not be denied its chance to speak, no matter what might come, no matter what questions remained unanswered and fears remained unassuaged.

"Don't you see?" She put her hand over her heart. "Right here, it's just *you*."

He stared at her for a good minute, shaking his head slightly. "God, what you do to me."

Watching her with eyes dark and intense under half-closed lids, he stroked the tips of his fingers along her jawline before trailing them down her throat and across her collarbone, his palm coming to rest over the hand on her breast in a caress that wrung a moan from her and warmed her throughout. Inside, she felt herself melt, going from solid to liquid to vapor, a misty cloud that rose up and up and up until she was spread out across the whole world. And yet the whole time she was still solid, still real, made so by his touch.

"Kiss me again," she implored.

Holden would not see her denied as his lips and tongue besieged hers in a shattering kiss. She yearned into him even more, and he took her, accommodating her softness against the planes of his hardness in the ageless melding of two bodies into one.

And for that fracture of a moment in time, Edie found surcease from her doubts. When he touched her, there was no thinking, only feeling. And whatever had been, whatever was to be, this connection was more powerful than it all.

"I *want* it to be just me," he murmured against her mouth. His hands drifted over her in exploration. "Only me."

"You are. I think you've always been." *Since the beginning of time.*

She felt his mouth curve upward in satisfaction as he slanted it in a new direction, his lips tugging at hers, and she lost herself anew in the feel of him.

Yes, there was a power between them. Holden hadn't named it, but she knew what it was: love. She loved him. Always had—since the beginning of time. And right now, with his mouth upon hers, with his arms holding her tight, she could believe he loved her, too.

But he'd said nothing about love.

Edie dropped her chin, breaking their kiss. Breathing hard, Holden let her, although his arms grew tighter around her.

"What is it?" he said urgently.

She had to know, now, while she still had a shred of reason. Now, when the force between them was its strongest and both their hearts could speak. "What about us, Holden?" she asked.

"What about us?"

"I know we've got this—" her fingers flexed against his chest "—between us, but is this all? Is there...more?"

She swallowed and made herself go on. "Because I need more, Holden. I-I need to know if I could be the one for you, too."

His eyes searched the depths of hers, and she felt as if her very soul was exposed to him.

"I won't lie to you, Edie," Holden finally said. "I still have a way to go in learning the kind of trust and faith that sort of commitment takes."

"And will you...ever?"

"I can't know that." His gaze fell away. "I can't make you promises, either. I seriously don't know if I can give you what you need. But I *do* know this is real between us."

He rested his forehead against hers. "I don't want it to stop, and I'm willing give it my best effort to make sure it doesn't."

Although it wasn't what she needed, still it was a lot for this man who'd been through so much. And she would have felt hopeful about the future of their relationship if his words hadn't seemed to come from a certain place in the distance, a position from which he felt safe to negotiate.

For even though he still held her, the bond between them waned, the gap widened.

She was losing him.

"But that's not enough," Edie said numbly. "Not for me."

"I know it isn't. I know it's not fair to you, either, to ask you to put that kind of trust in me." His face tightened in brief pain. "And I haven't got the best track record, have I, to convince you to take a chance on me. I mean, it's pretty obvious if it didn't happen with Rose after years of marriage…"

He seemed unable to finish, but Edie knew what he was getting at: if he'd held back from loving his wife, the mother of his child, with all his heart, then what chance did the two of them have together to find complete and absolute love? She wasn't going to be happy with anything less from him.

"I understand, Holden," Edie said, feeling sick in her soul. And empty, so very empty, when just a few moments ago she'd felt so complete. "But how can I give all of my love to a man who doesn't really believe there's a chance for us?"

"Now, I didn't say there was no chance—"

"You didn't, but you might as well have. *That* would have been complete honesty. Because face it, Holden, you're just not willing to take the risk of loving me with all your heart and soul!"

Oh, to be loved like that! It broke her own heart to wonder

if she would ever know such a love. Right now, it didn't seem possible, because if she couldn't find it with Holden, then she couldn't believe it was ever to be hers. She would never love another man as she loved him.

Or was it that she didn't love *him* enough—or trust him enough? There was still that fear having to do with him that lingered in the back of her mind. And held her back.

"Maybe...maybe it's just not meant to be between us, Holden," Edie said as she gently extracted herself from his embrace, stepping away from him. "And you can't make something like this happen just as you can't stop it from happening."

He must have heard the note of defeat in her voice, for he kept hold of her hand, their arms stretched between them. She tried to pull away. "Holden, please."

"No." He tightened his grip. "Edie. I *know* it's not fair to ask this, believe me. But don't give up on me, please. Not yet."

She looked at him pleadingly. Those words again, from her visions. She'd long ago stopped seeing the boy's face as he said them and saw instead only Holden's as he was now, though he was no less desperate.

She'd do anything for him, she really would, except accept less than what would make her happy.

"Holden, *please*," she almost begged. "Let me go. If you don't want all of me, if I can't have all of you, then let me go!"

They both jumped when the patio door slid open. Sam stood on the threshold with Beauty in his arms. He glanced from one to the other of them with concern. She could imagine what she and Holden looked like, poised like two adversaries in a tug-of-war across the breadth of an unbridgeable gap.

Holden dropped her hand. "What're you doing up, son?"

"Beauty was actin' like she had ta go again," he readily

explained. "I didn't want to get us in trouble if she had another accident."

"Well, let her give it a try," Holden told him.

The boy set the puppy down on the concrete and gave her a nudge toward the patch of grass beyond the patio, but it soon became obvious she hadn't the least need to do her business.

It occurred to Edie that the window to Sam's room was directly above the patio.

Her spring-loaded tail bouncing back and forth with each step like a metronome, Beauty sniffed around as if she'd caught the scent to something. But it only led her straight to Holden's feet, where she planted herself, head cocked and gazing up at him as if awaiting a cue from him.

"Looks like a false alarm," he said. "You'd best get back to bed, Sam. The real alarm will go off soon enough."

"'Kay." He heaved the pup into his arms, the too-long sleeves to his pajama top coming down over his hands and making her that much harder to hang on to.

Edie bent and helped him to get a better grip. He looked up at her with those gray-green eyes that had always done such a number on her heartstrings. She remembered the first time she'd stooped to look into them, as he cradled another precious burden to him. Although now it was she who stood bereft and forsaken.

Tears stung her eyes. "Good night, Sam—and maybe goodbye for a while, too."

"G'bye?"

"We're done with your PT, and it looks like Beauty's going to be staying here with you until you move to your new house, so we won't have much occasion to see each other." She brushed back his hair. "I-I'm going to miss you."

"But you're comin' to East Texas with us, aren't cha?" the boy asked.

Straightening in surprise, she shot Holden a glance. He looked extremely put out with himself.

"I haven't mentioned the matter to Edie yet, Sam," he said.

"Well, when will ya?" Sam asked bluntly.

Holden slanted his son a suspicious look and ran his hand through his hair. "When I talked to Tim Appleby," he explained to Edie, "he invited me to come visit East Texas, said a lot of people would like to see me again. He and his family would even put Sam and me up—and any other guests I might bring."

His mouth thinned. "Tonight when I tucked Sam in I told him we'd go—and promised him you would, too."

He shoved his fists into his pockets. "I can see now I shouldn't have made a promise I couldn't keep. Pretty hasty of me, I know."

"So will ya go with us?" Sam asked.

Edie didn't know what to say. Holden was clearly uncomfortable with the invitation—except he had been the one to broach it to Sam. Of course, that had also been before their conversation tonight.

She took in his tight-lipped expression, his stiff stance. He was definitely back to his closed-off, cynical self, and Edie feared it was because of her lack of trust in him being able to come through for her.

But it wasn't that, truly it wasn't! She just had to protect herself, because that unnamed danger was stronger and more powerful than ever. And it *did* center around him, even if she still didn't understand why or what it meant.

It just made her so afraid.

"C-can I let you know later, Sam?" she said to the boy. She didn't want to lie to him, but she didn't want him getting up false hopes, either. She didn't want that for any of them. "I mean, I'll have to see when you're going and check my calendar."

He didn't answer her but just looked at her more closely,

head cocked almost on the same angle as Beauty's. Then he did something totally out of character but completely wonderful. He put his arms around her waist, pressed his cheek to her middle and just hugged her for a long moment.

"I know you'll come if you can, Edie," he said, voice muffled against her shirtfront.

For a second, Edie was too stunned to respond. Then her arms went around the boy's shoulders as she bent over him and hugged him close.

She discovered a lump had lodged itself in her throat. She hadn't even known how much she'd hoped for such a spontaneous gesture from him, how well and truly it spoke of Sam's emotional recovery.

How she'd feared it wouldn't come about! Again her thoughts turned to that first time she'd seen him, having come fresh from a meeting with her supervisor about her needing to pull back and not get so emotionally involved with her patients. But she hadn't pulled back, and moments like these were her vindication and reward.

Of course, not always did she succeed. Sometimes, the failures were crushing. Yet she couldn't be any other way than how she was. Being this way required putting herself out there at risk more often, where some disappointment was inevitable. People would let you down; you'd let them down. But if you buried that vulnerable part of your nature in order to protect it, Edie knew, then you lost all ability to connect.

She had a feeling it was this life lesson that Sam was thanking her for teaching him.

Edie hugged him back, fiercely, by way of her thanks to him—for reminding her of that lesson.

She glanced up, and saw Holden standing alone, watching them. This change in Sam was due to his efforts and love, too. He hadn't given up, had come through when he needed to.

"Time for bed, Sam," he said, not ungently. "Go on, son."

Letting go of her, Sam picked up Beauty. "See you in the morning," he said to his father.

"See you in the morning," Holden echoed as the boy trotted off to bed.

Edie looked after him, so lost in her thoughts she didn't realize Holden had spoken to her until he'd reached the throat-clearing stage.

"Pardon?" she said, her mind still far away, her heart full.

"You don't have to go with us to East Texas, Edie, just to keep from letting Sam down. It's pretty clear he'll manage."

"Yes," she answered, then turned to Holden. "But will you?"

He arched one of those skeptical eyebrows at her. "I'm certainly not what you'd call jumping for joy at the thought of going back there again. But I thought it'd be good for Sam. I don't know, maybe good for me, too. Heaven knows—*you* know—I've still got a long way to go toward reconciling myself to all that happened there."

"But you were going to try?" Edie asked.

"Yes." His lower lip jutted pensively. He looked uncomfortable with revealing so much of himself.

"And you wanted me there with you?"

He gave an impatient shrug that made him seem that much more vulnerable. "I guess I had an idea in my mind that with you along, it'd be easier somehow. But of course I have no right to ask that of you."

Holden checked the time on his watch. "It's late," he said abruptly. Extending his hand, he indicated the door to the patio. "You're probably anxious to be on your way."

When she didn't move, he started toward the door without her. "I'll walk you to your car."

Still she remained where she was. Because suddenly, she wasn't anxious to be anywhere.

"Ask," Edie said.

That brought him around. "What?"

She clasped her hands behind her back to hide their shaking. "Ask me."

His face was as inscrutable as ever as he asked in a low voice, "So will you come to East Texas with us, Edie?"

Nothing had been solved between them, and perhaps nothing ever would. This wasn't about trust, either, because she had no more faith in a future for them than she'd had a few minutes ago. It was about something much bigger, much stronger.

Because again, heaven help her, she knew there was no way on earth she could deny this man all the love and support she could give him, no matter the risk to herself.

Maybe that was the danger she feared most of all.

"Yes, Holden, I'll come with you," Edie said.

Chapter Nine

Nothing had changed. The landscape was as lush and gently rolling, the towns they passed through as quaintly picturesque. Long-needled pines still lined the roadside, their green one of texture and depth, especially against the overcast sky, complex in its shades of pearl-gray.

It looked like rain, Holden thought with disappointment. He'd wanted the day to be bright and clear. Wanted Sam and Edie—and perhaps himself—to see this corner of the world in its best light.

"Are we almost there, Dad?" Sam asked from the back seat, which he and Beauty had taken over during the two-hour car ride from Dallas.

Holden glanced over his shoulder at them. After a morning of every kind of dog game Sam knew, the puppy had passed out cold, her chin resting on his denim-covered knee. His palm lay lovingly atop her shiny black head.

"Almost there," Holden answered. He shot a look across to the other occupant of the car. Edie's pure profile seemed cut from marble, in vivid contrast to the glowing, vibrant red-gold of the hair swirling around her shoulders. Her forearm lay on the console between them, her fingers curled into a fist of tension.

He knew the feeling.

He would have almost considered her consent to come on this trip a reprieve except for the fact that nothing had changed between them. And from the looks of it—and God knew he'd looked at it from every angle he could think of—nothing was bound to change soon. He knew he couldn't live with himself if he promised her a future he had no certainty he could make come true, and he knew that she was the kind of woman who wouldn't settle for less.

And she seemed to need that promise.

He wondered what continued to bother her about him that she couldn't go on the trust she espoused so fervently. Of course, maybe that was because he wanted her to trust him while still not quite giving all of his trust in return.

He could only hope that as time went on, he'd have the chance to ease those doubts and strengthen the bond between them. In fact, he almost reached over to twine his fingers through hers, to give her something real and solid to remind her of what they did have together. He needed it, wanted to hold on to her as he faced his boyhood home for the first time in twenty-four years. This wasn't going to be easy. Yet somehow he sensed that his making such contact with her might not be what was best for her right now.

Because when it came right down it, he wanted, more than anything else, what was best for Edie.

Holden was glad when they pulled off the main highway and up the long drive, coming to a stop in front of a cheery ranch house nestled in a grove of pine trees.

Tim Appleby and his family met them at the car, where introductions were made all around. They met Tim's wife, Annette, a shy, wholesome-faced woman, and his two boys, Trevor and Brent, one on either side of Sam, age-wise. Yet it was Tim's mother, Delia Appleby, a diminutive woman with hair of steel-wool gray, who came forward first, her black eyes fixed upon Holden as if he were an apparition.

She took his hand in her two fragile ones as she might have greeted an old friend. "Holden McKee. What a joy it is to see you again."

"Thank you." Holden smiled at her in puzzlement. "But I don't recall us meeting before."

"Oh, we haven't, not officially. It was at your daddy's funeral I first saw you—then at your mama's, a few years later."

He stiffened reflexively. He'd known he would be seeing people this weekend who'd not only remember him but his parents, too. Still, it was a strange feeling to have it happen. Like being abruptly dropped headfirst into the past.

An impression that Mrs. Appleby only continued to reinforce by saying, "I've always wondered what happened to that little boy who stood so straight and tall by his mama's casket. It nigh to tore my heart in pieces to think of you losing ever'one and ever'thing dear to you and havin' to go away."

Her words gave the memory new strength, and Holden found himself being towed down by it.

She's gone, son...gone...gone...gone....

Somehow, Delia's eyes pulled him back. "It didn't seem right you'd leave us, considerin' all your father had given to the community. He saved my Tim's life, you know. Although—" her soft voice grew softer as remembered pain flashed across her own features "—we lost Nell, the baby. That influenza was just too much for such a little thing."

Yes, even after twenty-four years, the ache of one's loss remained. Holden found himself squeezing Delia's hand with a murmured "I'm sorry."

"T'were a tragedy, to be sure. But you just thank the Lord for your blessings and go on, you know." Delia perked up. "Anyway, I'm real glad to know your daddy lives on in you.

You remind me of him so much, the way you look at a person—truly caring for another's affliction."

She fairly beamed at him, and the shadow of a few moments ago lifted. Holden smiled back, saying, "It's good to be back, Mrs. Appleby."

In fact, his heart felt fuller than it had in a long time, but in a fitting way. Perhaps the rest of this trip would be as nostalgic, rather than bring him the potential for real pain he still suspected it might.

"You know," Tim said suggestively, "we've got some good doctors around here, over in Tyler and Longview, but we could sure use one who was a part of the community."

Holden got the message, as he could see had Edie. Her brown eyes shone as she regarded him, as if to say how glad she was for him, pushing forward to make these discoveries, to garner these affirmations, to find out that he indeed had a place he belonged. No, it hadn't been an easy thing to do, coming to East Texas, but here he was, and what he'd found so far wasn't so very hard to manage after all.

Was this the place for him? Naturally, to set up practice here would mean he'd need some brushing up on general medicine—and a reorientation, psychologically. Treating people here would entail a whole different way of practicing medicine.

"I'll give the matter some thought," Holden told Tim. It was as much of a promise as he could give right now.

"Well, when you do," Tim added, with a significant look at Edie, who had been introduced both as Sam's physical therapist and a friend of the family, "remember, there're always opportunities for other health-care professionals here, too."

At that, her fine pale skin pinkened, and Holden was pulled into a reverie of another kind. About a whole different life—with Edie?

It hit him full force only then how much he would miss the support and understanding she gave so freely if they chose to part company. The future down that road yawned before him like an abyss.

Abruptly, Holden found himself wanting very badly to take the other road, toward the future with Edie. But something held him back from actually seeing it realized, and he wondered with some discouragement what it would take for him to.

It occurred to him that maybe there was one place he might find that out.

Unfortunately, the rest of the day passed in a blur of drop-in visits from old acquaintances, mostly of his parents. Sam was kept occupied by the Appleby boys, whom he took to instantly, and Edie, too, was taken in by Annette's East Texas hospitality.

Yet as the afternoon began to wane, Holden felt himself growing restless. The reunion dinner Tim had planned started at seven, and tomorrow there was a town social that would go on all day. If he didn't do it now, then he'd never have another chance.

Around half past three, he said, "Tim, would you and Annette mind keeping an eye on Sam while I slip away for a few hours? I want to see if I can find the stretch of riverbank I used to call mine."

Beside Holden, Edie made a sound of surprise.

"I don't mind at all," Tim replied. "Except I don't know as you'd recognize your old stompin' grounds. We've had nothing but rain the past few weeks and the river's as swollen as it gets nearly every spring." He peered at the overcast sky. "I wouldn't be surprised if we weren't in for a good downpour before dark."

"Sure, there's that chance, but I'd like to go there, anyway." Holden stood, and Edie came to her feet next to him.

"You're going to look for your box of memories, aren't you?" she said in a voice for his ears only.

He looked at her sharply, then remembered she'd been listening when he told Sam about his treasure box. "Yes. I think it's time I set some of those old memories to rest, if I can."

Her brown eyes were shining again, almost luminous, with her support. No, he didn't think he could live without it.

On a rush, before he could rethink the impulse, he asked, "Would you go with me?"

There was a flicker of doubt in the back of her gaze.

"I shouldn't have asked," Holden said quickly, feeling foolish. "This is probably something I need to do on my own, anyway."

"It's not that," Edie said. "I'd like to go. It's just that I'm not really much of a water person."

"Oh, we wouldn't go in the river." He wondered where she might have gotten that idea. "I wouldn't put either of us in that kind of danger."

She blinked, and he could see now that she was afraid. Her lower lip actually trembled. She wasn't just not a water person, she was downright scared of it.

He slid his hand into hers and squeezed. "Edie, this is one thing you can trust me on, really."

At his touch, she rallied, saying, "All right, I'll go with you." Although he could tell she still had her doubts.

But he wanted her to go there with him, to see into him in a way he could never verbalize. And maybe it would provide her with the reassurance about him she might be needing right now. Or perhaps she'd find the reason she couldn't trust him...and he'd lose her forever.

Either way, Holden knew, there was no turning back.

"This may turn out to be a wild-goose chase after all," Holden said as he craned his neck, looking for some sign of a landmark. He and Edie had been tramping a good half hour through low underbrush, the air around them thick with humidity and alive with the scent of pine. They'd had some rough going, mostly through mud and shallow water, but now they were deep into the piney woods where the ground was fairly dry, covered as it was by layers of pine needles and having been sheltered from the pounding rains Holden knew could wipe away a crop or wash out a road within a few hours.

He'd had to guess where to enter the woods, since his home was gone now, not even a wood pylon left from the pier-and-beam foundation to mark the house's place in his history. Yet he had spied familiar-looking pockets of forest and a certain decline in the topography, which had spurred him onward, Edie silent in his wake.

Now, though, he wasn't so sure it all hadn't been a lot of wishful thinking. Really, what did he hope to accomplish?

And why had he felt it so vital to have Edie along?

He glanced over at her as she took a break, leaning back against the rough-barked trunk of a pine. She looked tired. The farther they'd gone, the more she'd seemed to draw into herself.

She didn't need this, and he'd been selfish to ask her along.

"Maybe we should turn back," he said. "Now that I'm here and have had a look around, I think Tim's right. There's not much of a chance I'll find that hideout of mine or the box of mementos intact."

"What was in the box?" Edie asked, speaking for the first time since they'd started out.

"Oh, the typical things boys treasure—interesting rocks, that kind of thing...."

Sam had asked the same question, and for some reason, Holden found himself as reluctant now as he had been then to reveal all that he'd held dear within that box: a construction paper birthday card his mother had made for him when he'd turned six and money was too tight for them to afford a store-bought one; his dad's stethoscope, which only now did he remember cherishing—as he'd had a special hope to become a doctor some day, in honor of his father.

And at the bottom of the box, tucked in a corner, had been a curl of red-gold hair.

He pushed the toe of his shoe into the thick, pine-needle carpet. Yes, his boyhood hideout was probably permanently under water, the box containing the tokens of his life with his mother and father washed away long ago, making any search for it futile.

Was that why he'd fought so hard to keep from laying this part of his past to rest? Because standing here in this place, so close to the memories of his heart, he felt suddenly a failure, that he hadn't tried hard enough, somehow. That he hadn't trusted—or loved enough. Again.

And to try to do so seemed as futile and hopeless an endeavor as it had always seemed to him.

"God, I don't know, Edie..." he began, wanting to be truthful with her, this woman whose love and understanding had brought him to this point in time, and whom he now must turn away from if he truly wanted what was best for her, so she could find the happiness she deserved.

But she interrupted him with an awed "Look, Holden! Isn't it beautiful?"

He was compelled to raise his eyes up, and he beheld the familiar view he had also once cherished, that of diffused light filtering down among the verdant branches. It was almost like sitting in a church, with the sweeping height of the trees making a vaulted ceiling and the light filtering down as if through a stained-glass window.

Then his vision focused on a familiar sight. Of course. Had he actually forgotten those two pines whose forked trunks crossed? *"X" marked the spot.*

"I know where we are now," he said. He squinted into the foliage and saw the overgrown path to the left. "Follow me."

Holden didn't wait to see if Edie followed but took off through the underbrush. Could it be he'd actually find that special place of his after all these years? And perhaps then he would be allowed to find peace at last.

He could smell the river now, hear it rushing past. He broke through one last layer of prickly growth and into a small clearing. The riverbank lay not twenty feet away, straight ahead. He strode up to it, knowing before he took each step how it would feel beneath the soles of his shoes.

At the edge, the ground sheared off at a rugged fifty-degree angle, heading down to a narrow rocky strip that followed right along the water. Cautiously, Holden descended the muddy incline and searched the bank downstream with his gaze.

"Edie, this is it," he said excitedly. Now that he was here, he couldn't help but feel an immanency about the moment. "The hideout was underneath an overhang of bank that used to flood about once every four springs. And from the looks of it, this might be one of those springs. But you never know. You just never know—"

He turned eagerly to find Edie standing at the edge of the incline, her brown eyes dark and disturbed.

"Edie?" he said.

She didn't seem to hear him as she stared past him at the river. She was eerily still but trembling in a way that made her appear poised to bolt at any moment.

"Edie, what's wrong?" Holden asked with a trace of alarm. "Is it being close to the water? You don't have to stand so near, you know—"

"I don't like this place," she said hoarsely, her gaze unblinking and almost mesmerized. "I don't think we should be here. It's...dangerous."

"Sure, the river's up, but I know this part of it like the back of my hand. And don't worry, I'm not going to go in the water."

She continued her almost vigilant watch. Holden turned to look in the direction of her gaze and saw nothing except the gushing brown water. Yes, the river was running high. His hideout *was* likely under water. But he only wanted to see if it was still there. He wasn't a brash ten-year-old this time; he wouldn't do anything to endanger either of them....

Holden reeled back around. Edie hadn't moved a muscle. Indeed, she seemed a statue, although around her swirled her hair, that living mantle of red-gold, shimmering like armor in the colorless light....

He saw it then as all surrounding detail faded to nothing, his vision becoming sharp and surreal as he beheld her terrified stance, the soul-shattering confusion in her eyes.

In his ears was the sound of his heartbeat and a low thrumming like bees.

It couldn't be. Edie was...was...Elsa?

Holden's world split in two, chaos boiling up out of the chasm created. *It couldn't be.* It couldn't be. What possible reason could there be for such a bizarre twist of fate?

No! It was merely this place. Here was where he'd lost the only loved one he might have had a chance at saving.

Except she'd had to save *his* life—because of his foolish wish to go after the treasure box. He had put them both into danger, and he had failed to rescue her.

But if I'd have known how alone I'd feel after she died, I would have done it, no matter the risk. The words echoed in his mind, those which he'd said to Edie.

That was it. That was what remained unresolved in his subconscious, what had brought him here, and he was simply transferring some of that sense of failure with Elsa—or maybe his failure with Rose—to his relationship with Edie. This...this completely *absurd* notion was all in his mind! It had to be.

But bits and pieces of impressions came back to him: Edie telling Sam her name was not E.D., that the name had come to her mother in a dream when she was pregnant... Edie's birthday—he did a quick calculation—which had fallen nine full months to the day from that awful moment when he'd lost both his mother and his faithful companion... The impact of her strength of presence and how it had hit him gut-deep... Those first moments with her when he'd looked into her eyes and felt that wrinkle in time, showing him two possible paths he might take, two possible perceptions, one of which he might reach out and grasp, and one he must turn away from...

And now her fear of the river.

So was *that* the root of Edie's basic distrust of him—he'd been unable to rescue her, unable to keep her safe, unable to love her enough, even after she risked everything for him?

And if they could not have that soul-deep level of trust, then there was no hope for them to be together.

Damn it, he shouldn't have come back here, should have left the past alone!

His head was throbbing with trying to sort out all the thoughts spinning around it when another stunning possibility struck him: *Did Edie know?*

He glanced up at her. She was still staring beyond him to the river coursing past. Something told Holden that she didn't know—which gave him hope that this realization was all in his head, despite what his instincts might be telling him. Although she was the one with the instincts like a bloodhound—

Suddenly, a great surge of urgency enveloped him. If it *was* true, he didn't want her to know, and not merely because of his having failed her those years ago. But for Edie—so brave, so loyal, so completely hopeful. Even Edie would have trouble coming to terms with and trusting in the meaning of such a development.

No, Holden didn't want her to know, for he realized he'd be unable to make her any assurances, either. And she would need assurances, badly. As much as Sam had. But unlike with his son, Holden didn't think he'd be able to convince her to trust and believe in the meaning of such a circumstance, even if he didn't know what that meaning might be. Because right now Holden didn't trust or believe in himself.

And then he *would* lose her...this time forever.

The fear was overwhelming, paralyzing. Even though she'd always been uncomfortable around water, this was different. The feeling of suffocating panic clawed at her throat in a way she couldn't be rational about, worse than it had been that evening she stepped into the creek. All she could think about was that she had to get away from here—and fast. Danger whirled all around her, a maelstrom of menace, just as it had in her vision. Danger—for her.

Edie turned and ran.

Branches bruised her forearms as she pushed them out of the way, their sharp nodes scraping her skin. Her breath seemed trapped in her chest, and she gasped for air around dry sobs of terror.

She became aware of Holden calling her name. *Just as he had in her vision.* Only it wasn't Holden the boy, but Holden the man. The man she loved, had always loved. Would always love. Whatever had happened or might happen, she couldn't turn away from him even if her life depended upon it.

Edie stumbled, slowed and sank to her knees. It struck her what posture she was in, that of a supplicant. And she'd have prayed if she only knew what to pray for.

A moment later she was grasped by the shoulders and hauled into a pair of strong arms.

Edie grabbed onto that strength, her fingers digging into Holden's shoulders as she blinked rapidly, fighting for sanity. His face swam into view and she could see he was deathly pale, his eyes gone black with his own dread—of what?

She began to shiver uncontrollably.

"Holden... Oh, Holden, I don't know why, but I'm just so afraid!"

"Then let's leave," he said, his face grim. "There's nothing here so important I'd make you stay."

"But this *place* is important to you. Finding that hideout and your box of memories is important, if you're ever going to release yourself from that part of your past—"

"No!" He almost shouted the word. His jaw clamped shut as he himself obviously fought for control. The sight allayed her apprehension not one bit.

"No," he said more calmly. "I don't need to find anything. I don't need to go there. Not anymore." He brushed her hair back with both hands, taking her face between them. "I know everything I need to right now."

She wanted to believe him—God knew she did—but she could see he was struggling, too, with some impression about this place. And it disturbed him greatly.

It had taken so much courage for him to come here, and now he would leave before resolving what he needed to because of her.

Edie withdrew from his embrace, standing on shaky legs that threatened to buckle. "You go, then, Holden. Go and see if you can find what you're looking for. I-I'll wait here."

Her voice trembled. It wasn't how she would have had it happen—she wanted to be with him every step of the way— but it was the best she could do right now.

Holden studied her, his gray-green eyes filled with a thousand reservations. "No," he said again. "No, I won't leave you here alone, not when you're feeling so threatened."

"I didn't say I was feeling threatened." She swallowed uneasily, her gaze pinned on his shirtfront, and forced herself to admit, "but I have to tell you, Holden, there is something about this place that makes me feel in danger of...of *you.*"

He said nothing for a moment. Then he swore under his breath, violently. And dragged her back into his arms to possess her mouth with his.

As ever, his kiss overwhelmed her, although it was nothing

about power and surrender, and everything about giving and wanting their all from each other.

By the time he lifted his head, she was trembling and clinging to him for a different reason.

Still, Edie couldn't let the matter slide. It was too important to them both.

"What about searching out the truth?" she whispered. She pressed one palm to his chest. "Holden, you know how important it is to keep looking into your heart for it, to work through the pain in your past so you can go on freely."

It occurred to her such a reminder was for herself as much as him.

There was another hesitation from him as his gaze delved into hers, then it shuttered in that old way he had of closing himself off from the pain. And from her.

"Actually, I think I've unearthed quite enough of my past for today," he said with that ironic lift of one eyebrow. "We're leaving here, right now."

She knew better than to argue with him when he spoke with such finality. And for once she didn't have the courage to pursue the subject, to make either of them dig too much more deeply into matters that at this moment seemed so acutely painful she couldn't comprehend how either she or Holden would ever get to the bottom of them and be free at last.

Edie fell into step beside Holden as he led them out of the woods and back to the dirt road where his car waited, her tread heavy. Oh, why couldn't she be stronger? She felt certain she would lose him if she couldn't face this danger and discover its source.

It would always be between them, the one time when she hadn't trusted—or loved enough.

Chapter Ten

He didn't know how he was going to make it through the evening.

Holden slid his dress shirt on, the sleeves sticking to his damp shoulders, and stared at himself in the steamed-around-the-edges mirror in Tim Appleby's guest bathroom.

Yes, there he was, the same Holden McKee who'd looked back at him since he was old enough to recognize his reflection, be it in a mirror or window or pool of water. And yet, it was just a reflection, not reality. Not literally.

Maybe none of this was.

What was going on here? Was it all in his mind, this sensation that he had known Edie in wholly different circumstances, so to speak? And what if he had? How did that change anything—if possible, wouldn't it make the situation between them better?

It might, if he could just be certain his and Edie's presence in each other lives right now was meant for the good. And how could that be, if he'd betrayed her trust in him so grievously? How could it be if she felt herself in danger around him—and with good reason?

He ran his hand over his face, needing to feel the very corporeal texture of his skin. Edie was real. He'd touched her, held her, kissed her. And it had been real.

Holden tried to concentrate on buttoning his shirt, but his mind had other ideas. That was it—maybe this whole realization about Edie *was* all in his mind, a projection of his culpability and the inability to deal with it within himself. Maybe it wasn't about Edie at all.

And if so, then he was getting very deep into his subconscious indeed. What was he still trying desperately to avoid coming to terms with? He had to be honest, had to look for the truth. There was no choice in the matter now. But would knowing the truth tear Edie from him—again?

He didn't know how he'd go on this time if it did.

What about Edie? What was she going through right now? He'd seen how terrified she'd been upon being in the place where she *supposedly* had lost her life. But it seemed that whatever possibility had occurred to him, it had yet to strike her. And what would happen when it did? She already recognized the danger he was—had been—to her.

So she'd been right not to trust him, all along. And damn, that hurt! It nearly destroyed him.

Holden took a deep breath and made a distracted attempt at tying his tie. And he made a decision: she never had to know. The two of them would attend this function tonight and leave straight away tomorrow morning. Neither of them would ever have to return to East Texas ever again. He'd make her the promises she needed from him. By God, he'd make *himself* believe she could trust him completely, would make her believe, too. She wanted to, he could see that.

But the real truth would always be there between them.

Holden yanked the unmanageable tie off, popping a button on his collar. He swore in frustration when he couldn't find the tiny pearl-white button on the busily patterned linoleum floor. He'd have to get a safety pin from Annette if he couldn't locate one in his bag.

He made his way down the hall to the bedroom he and Sam were sharing this weekend and had rummaged through his hanging bag for a full five minutes before he realized he hadn't heard the door to Edie's bedroom open. He thought surely she'd have heard him vacate the bathroom.

Holden opened his door to find Beauty sitting just outside of it. She wagged her tail at the sight of a familiar face. For a moment, he found himself scrutinizing hers warily before he caught himself. Good grief, she was just a puppy!

"What're you doing loose in the house?" he asked. He'd have to find Sam and give him a talking to about being a proper guest and not letting one's animals roam his host's home unattended. First, though, he had a need to hear the reassuring sound of Edie's voice telling him she was still the woman he'd held in his arms and felt that powerful connection with, that she had every hope, every belief, that they would continue to find such a bond together.

He stepped across the hall and knocked softly. "Edie? Bathroom's all yours if you want it." She'd deferred the first shower to him, which had seemed strange, only because most women usually wanted a little more time to get ready than a man did, even if Edie didn't seem the type who did a lot of primping.

Just give her hair a brush and she was ready to go.

He closed his eyes on a muttered oath of self-censure. He must be insane to even contemplate believing what he did. It had to be the fact of being here in this place for the first time in twenty-four years. He *was* having some sort of a regressive experience or something, as little as he gave credence to such theories. Anything, though, would be better than this feeling which sat like a cold, hard rock in his gut.

Holden knocked again. "Edie?"

No answer. Beauty sniffed at the doorjamb, then whined softly.

He turned the doorknob. Looked around the room.

It was empty.

Holden took off down the hall to the front door at a dead run. He didn't need a canine's nose to know where Edie had gone.

She had little trouble finding her way back to the same spot on the riverbank for someone who'd only been this way once before.

Edie took a tentative step forward, to within only a few feet from the edge of the embankment. Her gaze searched the depths of the flowing water even as she wondered what she sought there.

She only knew she had to try to figure this out somehow. She couldn't go back to Holden not having faced this still unnamed, unidentified fear.

Yet what if she was unable to? How could she expect him to give his all to her if she wasn't able to do the same? And she still wanted that kind of all-encompassing love with him. She didn't think she'd be able to live without it. And she knew she couldn't live with anything less.

It started to rain, a pattering down between leaves and branches that quickly grew to a steady downpour. Was it her imagination or had the level of the river risen just in the few hours since she'd stood here with Holden?

She'd have given anything to leave, but she seemed to be caught between two forces, one that pulled her toward the river and the answer to what the danger was, and one that tugged her away from it and into the safety of Holden's arms. But he was the source of the danger! She'd felt it in her visions.

Edie made herself stare into the river, so hard tears came to her eyes. They fell, too, because it hurt inside. What could make her stop loving him? She couldn't fathom it. She would always love him, with all her heart and soul. Had always loved him, since the beginning of time.

But the danger was growing by the second, filling her, torturing her—

Then she spied it. Blinking the moisture from her eyes, Edie could see something wedged in the crook of a half-submerged tree in the middle of the river. It was definitely square and clearly not of nature, for it shone dully under a patina of dirt and muck.

It looked like a box. *Holden's box.*

Edie pressed her fingers to her trembling lips as even more tears coursed down her cheeks—not of despair, but of relief, of thanks. Of hope. This was why she'd had to come back here! She must have known it somehow. Oh, to be able to take that box back to Holden, to give him back those memories that would allow him to get past the hurt of his losses here and remember those he lost with love.

Except she still had to venture into the river to get it.

It was moving rapidly, but she told herself it didn't look that deep. And there were plenty of trees to provide handholds along the way. She'd simply feel her way along, and if the water got too deep or the current too strong, she'd turn around and come back the way she'd gone.

She sat on the edge of the bank and cautiously made her way feet first down the slope, bumpy with gnarled tree roots and protruding rock. Up close, the churning dark water looked no less ominous. Before she could think about it, Edie took off one shoe and stuck her toes into the water, yanking them back almost instantaneously as if she expected to be burned. But she wasn't. In fact, as she eased her whole foot back in, she was surprised at how moderate the water temperature turned out to be. This might not be such a scary undertaking after all.

She took off her other shoe and stepped into the water, sliding each foot forward a little at a time, her toes sinking into the soft mud in a not unpleasant sensation. The water flowed around her ankles, then her knees, then her thighs as she crept deeper into the river.

When she had gone in to waist-high, it seemed the current became stronger, her footing a little less maintainable. That uncontrollable panic raised the hair on the back of her neck. Edie found a resting place against the downstream side of large gum tree and caught her breath. She must get control of her fear! For Holden. For Holden, she could do this. And once she had, nothing would stand in the way of their love.

The box was only another fifteen feet away.

Clinging to the tree trunk, Edie felt for a firm spot to place her next step. Still holding on to a large limb of the gum tree, she stretched for the closest branch of the next. Only one after that and she'd reach the box. She was so close!

Grasping a thin branch, the only one she could reach, she took another step. But her foot met nothing, the branch broke off in her hand. And Edie went under with a splash.

Pure hysteria seized her, surrounded her in a snare that had her pawing at her face in a frenzy, choking on her sobs of panic. *No!* her mind screamed. *This can't be happening.*

Her lungs felt as if they'd collapse at any moment.

She must have come upon some sort of a drop-off to the river bottom, for there was no light above her. That's how deep she was. She was going to drown!

Edie kicked madly, now out of control, but her feet met only slick mud beneath them.

Was this how it would end, her drowning in this river and never knowing what it was like to love Holden McKee with all of her heart and soul, have him love her back the same way, after being so close, so very, very close?

No! It couldn't end like this!

Edie's toes stubbed on a hard outcropping on the river's floor. She used it to push off mightily, which sent her speeding upward in a surge. Encouraged, she clawed her way to the surface, arms windmilling desperately.

She came up gasping and sputtering, her hair blinding her for a moment until she shoved it out of her eyes. Directly in front of her was a crook in the tree's trunk. Wedged in it was Holden's box.

With a grunt of effort, she heaved herself upward on the tree trunk, hand outstretched.

And the box was hers.

Holden crashed through the bushes just in time to see Edie go under. He hesitated not a moment but plunged into the river after her.

Yet the current was strong. Before he had a chance even to get his bearings, his feet were swept from under him and he was carried thirty feet downstream in the chest-high water. His hand automatically shot out and grabbed at a passing branch, then another. The third try he caught one and held on.

Anxiously, he searched for the spot he'd last seen Edie's bright hair in the water. Where was it? Raindrops obstructed his vision, and he dashed them out of his eyes, cursing the infernal East Texas weather as he did so.

He hauled himself half a foot higher on the trunk and looked again, trying not to panic, not to give up hope.

He saw nothing but brown water and brown tree trunks under the dull slate gray of the overcast sky.

Then up out of the water she shot, head and shoulders clearing the surface in a powerful lunge. Her arms wrapped around a tree right in front of her. She thrust her hair clear of her eyes, which fixed upon some object resting in the fork of the tree. She seized it like a precious treasure.

It couldn't be. Was it really...his box?

"Edie!" Holden yelled.

It was the wrong thing to do. Startled, she jerked around

and lost her grip on her anchor. The current immediately swept her up and carried her along.

"Grab something!" Holden screamed, but before she could she collided with another sturdy tree half submerged in the river. He heard her cry of pain, yet she stuck to it—just barely. She was severely hampered, he could see, by trying to keep hold of the box. Holding on to it for him.

She glanced around in a frenzy until she located him. Her large brown eyes were full of foreboding.

"Holden!" She gulped and tried to smile. "Do you see what I've found?"

"Yes," he answered, although he wanted nothing less right now than that collection of memories—among them a red-gold lock of hair. It almost seemed a veritable Pandora's box: best left alone rather than opened with any intention, even good.

Or did she know already?

Then Holden forgot all about the box. Adrenaline spurted through his body, making his extremities tingle. There, just over Edie's head, a cottonmouth skulked—and laid its deadly plans.

With lightning calculation, he assessed the situation. On the good side, Edie's short junket had put her within ten feet of him, although not directly downstream. It would be a stretch, but with just the right timing, he might be able to catch hold of her hand once she let go of her mooring. He could get them to the bank from there.

And if he missed, she'd be lost down the river. Again.

He couldn't let himself think of such a possibility.

"Edie," Holden called over the rushing water, making his voice as assured and calm as possible, "I need for you to push off from that tree, hard as you can, straight toward me. I'm going to angle myself out from this trunk toward you so I can catch you. Okay?"

Her face filled with doubt. "I-I don't know. I think I can hold on here for quite a while, maybe till the water recedes."

"But it's only going to get higher with this rain. Believe me, I know this river."

"Then...then I'll climb higher."

She actually hitched herself up a notch on the trunk. In sheer horror, Holden watched the snake uncoil itself from the branch not three feet above her.

This could not be happening! he thought wildly. What kind of God was so cruel and unfeeling as to do this to him—to do this to her *again?* Would he fail her again? He didn't think he could go on if he did.

Yet he knew at once that why ever he'd come to this place at this moment in time, he had chosen this path. And it was up to him to decide what the outcome would be this time.

"Edie, no, you've got to let go," he said. "I'll catch you."

"But what about the box?"

She *would* argue! "Let go of it."

She bit her lower lip. "But, Holden, it's so important to you, and now that I have it in my hands—"

The snake twisted and twined around the limb. Its dark-brown head dropped and floated in the air like a specter.

"Let go of the box," Holden commanded. "Now!"

"I know—I'll reach up and see if I can wedge it into a crook in this tree so we can get it later—"

"No!" He didn't want her getting one inch closer to that snake, didn't want her looking up and into that vampire face. "No, don't, Edie! Let it go! It doesn't matter, really it doesn't. Just push off and concentrate on grabbing for my hand."

A war of indecision was still being waged in her brown eyes.

He grasped the strong limb above him with one hand and reached out with the other. "Trust me, Edie," he implored her, and tried not to let a niggling of doubt slither its sinister way into his brain the way that snake was stealthily inching closer to her.

Still she wavered. The snake hovered lower.

"Edie, for the love of heaven, let go!" Holden shouted.

Please, he begged, *please, I can't lose her. Don't let me lose her. Don't let me let her down. Not again. It doesn't matter how or why we've been brought together. Just don't let me go through the rest of my life without her.*

Then the one assurance that would make the difference to them both popped into his head.

"I love you, Edie," Holden vowed. "I've always loved you, and I always will, with all my heart and soul. *I promise you that on my life.*"

He put everything into his gaze, faith and hope and trust. And most of all love.

The snake reared back, a split second from striking.

She thrust the box away from her. At the same time, she launched herself toward him, arms and legs thrashing.

The water churned, splashing into his eyes and blinding him. He hadn't time to wipe them. Every moment counted.

Holden kept Edie's last position in his mind's eye and levered himself out and away from the tree, arm outstretched, hand extended, fingers spread—and grabbing at nothing but water.

He squinted but could see nothing. Had she gone under?

"Don't you dare do it," he screamed. "Don't you *dare* give up on me!"

Then something brushed his fingertips. He stretched his arm to the breaking point, his hand clutching, clasping, grasping, reaching as he had never reached for anything in his life—

And finally finding her slender fingers with his.

Holden grabbed onto them and held, the jerk on his arm almost pulling his shoulder from its socket as the current dragged at them both. With one last groan of effort, he pulled her to him and to safety.

He blinked urgently and found Edie with his gaze. Her hair was a dreadful tangle. Mud streaked her face as she looked up at him. But she was safe. At last.

Within minutes he'd maneuvered them to the river's edge and up the embankment, where he enveloped her in his arms.

Tears collected in his eyes. How good it felt to hold her! There was nothing more real than this.

Holden lifted Edie's chin and kissed her passionately. "Don't you ever, *ever* leave me again," he rasped.

"Again?" she asked, clearly puzzled.

He stared at her. *Had* it all been his imagining, some sort of subconscious attempt to try to make sense of what had happened in his life so he could come to terms with it? Or was it in his believing in what seemed impossible that his own renewal of hope and love could be born?

Edie gazed at him with such shining trust and love, it took his breath away.

It didn't matter. All that mattered was that they had found each other, through their efforts, however hampered by doubt and fears. Still they had pressed on—and believed.

"What I meant is, now that we've found each other," Holden explained, "I don't ever want to be apart again."

Her smile was radiant, as if he'd just given her the most precious gift in the world. And perhaps he had.

"I love you, Holden McKee," she murmured. "More than I can say."

"And I love you, Edie Turner, more than you'll ever know," he answered.

Holden pulled Edie close, cherishing the feeling of her safe in his arms, as a peace came over him, pure and rich, like nothing he'd ever felt in his life. But then, never had he witnessed the power of such a love that had been at work today, making every heartache he'd ever endured in this life worth the pain.

"Hey, look what's happened!" Edie exclaimed.

Holden opened his eyes. The rain had stopped, and the clouds parted to reveal just a patch of blue at first, then an expanse as wide as a river through which the setting sun poured like butterscotch, coating the raindrops still clinging to the trees and filling them with light from within, like thousands of prisms.

His heart expanded so much he thought his chest would burst. "I wish Sam was here," he said huskily. "It almost feels like you *could* reach up, like so, and touch heaven."

"But don't you already know?" Edie kissed the edge of his jaw. "Heaven's not up there. It's all around you. It always has been."

And as Holden bent his head to take her lips to his, he sent a prayer of thanks sailing upward, for it occurred to him, actually, that he held heaven in his arms.

With a sigh of satisfaction, God sat back in his radiant throne.

"You're welcome, my son," he murmured, a beatific smile touching his lips. "You're entirely welcome."

* * * * *

**Coming this September 1999
from SILHOUETTE BOOKS
and bestselling author**

RACHEL LEE

CONARD COUNTY:
Boots & Badges

Alicia Dreyfus—a desperate woman on the run—is about to discover that she *can* come home again...to Conard County. Along the way she meets the man of her dreams—and brings together three other couples, whose love blossoms beneath the bold Wyoming sky.

Enjoy four complete, **brand-new** stories in one extraordinary volume.

Available at your favorite retail outlet.

Silhouette®

Look us up on-line at: http://www.romance.net

PSCCBB

If you enjoyed what you just read,
then we've got an offer you can't resist!

Take 2 bestselling love stories FREE!

Plus get a FREE surprise gift!

Clip this page and mail it to Silhouette Reader Service™

IN U.S.A.	IN CANADA
3010 Walden Ave.	P.O. Box 609
P.O. Box 1867	Fort Erie, Ontario
Buffalo, N.Y. 14240-1867	L2A 5X3

YES! Please send me 2 free Silhouette Romance® novels and my free surprise gift. Then send me 6 brand-new novels every month, which I will receive months before they're available in stores. In the U.S.A., bill me at the bargain price of $2.90 plus 25¢ delivery per book and applicable sales tax, if any*. In Canada, bill me at the bargain price of $3.25 plus 25¢ delivery per book and applicable taxes**. That's the complete price and a savings of over 10% off the cover prices—what a great deal! I understand that accepting the 2 free books and gift places me under no obligation ever to buy any books. I can always return a shipment and cancel at any time. Even if I never buy another book from Silhouette, the 2 free books and gift are mine to keep forever. So why not take us up on our invitation. You'll be glad you did!

215 SEN CNE7
315 SEN CNE9

Name _____ (PLEASE PRINT)

Address _____ Apt.# _____

City _____ State/Prov. _____ Zip/Postal Code _____

* Terms and prices subject to change without notice. Sales tax applicable in N.Y.
** Canadian residents will be charged applicable provincial taxes and GST.
All orders subject to approval. Offer limited to one per household.
® are registered trademarks of Harlequin Enterprises Limited.

SROM99 ©1998 Harlequin Enterprises Limited

THE FORTUNES OF TEXAS

This BRAND-NEW program includes 12 incredible stories about a wealthy Texas family rocked by scandal and embedded in mystery.

It is based on the tremendously successful *Fortune's Children* continuity.

Membership in this family has its privileges...and its price.

But what a fortune can't buy, a true-bred Texas love is sure to bring!

This exciting program will start in September 1999!

Available at your favorite retail outlet.

Silhouette®

Look us up on-line at: http://www.romance.net

PSFOTGEN

*This August 1999, the legend
continues in Jacobsville*

DIANA PALMER

LOVE WITH A LONG, TALL TEXAN

A trio of brand-new short stories featuring
three irresistible Long, Tall Texans

**GUY FENTON, LUKE CRAIG
and CHRISTOPHER DEVERELL...**

This August 1999, Silhouette brings readers an
extra-special collection for Diana Palmer's legions
of fans. Diana spins three unforgettable stories of
love—Texas-style! Featuring the men you can't get
enough of from the wonderful town of Jacobsville,
this collection is a treasure for all fans!

*They grow 'em tall in the saddle in Jacobsville—and
they're the best-looking, sweetest-talking men to be
found in the entire Lone Star state. They are proud,
hardworking men of steel and it will take
the perfect woman to melt their hearts!*

**Don't miss this collection of original
Long, Tall Texans stories...available in
August 1999 at your favorite retail outlet.**

Silhouette®

Look us up on-line at: http://www.romance.net

PSLTTT

Silhouette ROMANCE™

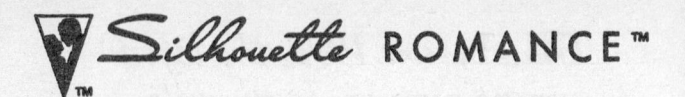

Join *Silhouette Romance* as more couples experience the joy only babies can bring!

Bundles of Joy

September 1999
THE BABY BOND
by Lilian Darcy (SR #1390)

Tom Callahan a daddy? Impossible! Yet that was before Julie Gregory showed up with the shocking news that she carried his child. Now the father-to-be knew marriage was the answer!

October 1999
BABY, YOU'RE MINE
by Lindsay Longford (SR #1396)

Marriage was the *last* thing on Murphy Jones's mind when he invited beautiful—and pregnant—Phoebe McAllister to stay with him. But then she and her newborn bundle filled his house with laughter...and had bachelor Murphy rethinking his no-strings lifestyle....

And in December 1999, popular author

MARIE FERRARELLA

brings you

THE BABY BENEATH THE MISTLETOE (SR #1408)

Available at your favorite retail outlet.

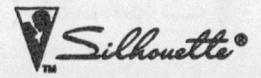

Silhouette®

Look us up on-line at: http://www.romance.net

SRBOJS-D

SILHOUETTE BOOKS
is proud to announce the arrival of

THE BABY OF THE MONTH CLUB:

BABY TALK

the latest installment of author
Marie Ferrarella's
popular miniseries.

When pregnant Juliette St. Claire met Gabriel Saldana than she discovered he wasn't the struggling artist he claimed to be. An undercover agent, Gabriel had been sent to Juliette's gallery to nab his prime suspect: Juliette herself. But when he discovered her innocence, would he win back Juliette's heart and convince her that he was the daddy her baby needed?

Don't miss Juliette's induction into
THE BABY OF THE MONTH CLUB
in September 1999.

Available at your favorite retail outlet.

Silhouette®

Look us up on-line at: http://www.romance.net

PSBOTMC

Silhouette ROMANCE™

VIRGIN BRIDES

Your favorite authors tell more heartwarming stories of lovely brides who discover love... for the first time....

July 1999 GLASS SLIPPER BRIDE
Arlene James (SR #1379)

Bodyguard Jack Keller had to protect innocent Jillian Waltham—day and night. But when his assignment became a matter of temporary marriage, would Jack's hardened heart need protection...from Jillian, his glass slipper bride?

September 1999 MARRIED TO THE SHEIK
Carol Grace (SR #1391)

Assistant Emily Claybourne secretly loved her boss, and now Sheik Ben Ali had finally asked her to marry him! But Ben was only interested in a temporary union...until Emily started showing him the joys of marriage—and love....

November 1999 THE PRINCESS AND THE COWBOY
Martha Shields (SR #1403)

When runaway Princess Josephene Francoeur needed a short-term husband, cowboy Buck Buchanan was the perfect choice. But to wed him, Josephene had to tell a *few* white lies, which worked...until "Josie Freeheart" realized she wanted to love her rugged cowboy groom forever!

Available at your favorite retail outlet.

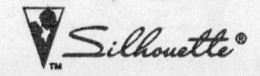

Silhouette®

Look us up on-line at: http://www.romance.net

SRVB992